EARL CRAZY

ANNA BRADLEY

OLIVER-HEBER BOOKS

CHAPTER
ONE

HAMPSTEAD HEATH, LONDON EARLY
SPRING, 1815

A man's wits were an ephemeral thing, and apt to abandon him at the least provocation.

Kit's had fled somewhere along the road from Kent to London. He couldn't say for certain where it had happened, but by the time he arrived at Prestwick Cottage, they were nowhere to be found.

Otherwise, he would have known better than to open his front door. He would have realized, before his fingertips touched the door knob, what he was likely to find on the other side.

Or rather, *who*.

"Well, Prestwick? Do you mean to keep me standing out here all night?" Darby slouched against the door frame, one dark eyebrow quirked. "Or are you going to invite me inside?"

That was the question, wasn't it? On the one hand, Darby was a good fellow, despite being an unrepentant rake, but on the other hand... Darby was an unrepentant rake, despite being a good fellow.

Not that Kit objected to rakes. If a gentleman chose to haunt London's seamy underbelly, as he'd done himself for the better part of the last six years, he did so knowing he couldn't stir a step without stumbling over some grinning rogue or other.

Scandalous rakes were all very well in their proper place, at the proper time.

But Kit's doorstep wasn't the proper place. Not anymore.

"*Well*, Prestwick?"

"Give me a moment. I'm trying to decide."

Darby straightened with a huff. "That's a fine welcome for your oldest friend. For God's sake, you can't mean to leave me out here. I'll catch my death in this cold."

"Let it be a lesson to you, Darby, not to turn up uninvited," Kit grumbled, but he was already waving Darby inside. "How did you find me?"

"By the most ingenious method imaginable. You see, you're the Earl of Prestwick, and this..." Darby waved a dramatic hand around the entryway. "Is Prestwick House. And here you are. Astonishing, it is not?"

The Earl of Prestwick. He should be accustomed to the title by now, but after a year, it still hung awkwardly on him, like an ill-fitting tailcoat. "This isn't Prestwick House. It's the cottage."

"So it is." Darby glanced around the cramped entryway, but when no servant appeared, he tossed his coat, hat and walking stick on a nearby table. "Hiding, are you?"

"Not very well, it seems." He might have known Darby would waste no time finding him. He'd arrived in London mere hours earlier, but Darby was nothing if not resourceful. "You may as well have a brandy, now you're here."

"Ah, that's better, Prestwick. For a moment I was

worried you'd turned into an utter savage after such a long time in the country." Darby followed him into the study, and threw himself into a chair near the fire. "How was Kent? As dull as ever?"

"Kent was quiet." Too quiet.

"London isn't." Darby accepted the glass of brandy Kit held out to him. "Just as well, too. I daresay you're dying for some amusement, after a year of rusticating."

Rusticating? Was that how the *ton* referred to mourning now? It was admittedly a distressing word, one that conjured up all sorts of unpleasantness, and the *ton* did prefer to avoid unpleasantness. "I didn't return to London for amusement, Darby."

"You're likely to find it, whether you want it or not, but very well, Prestwick. Why did you return, if not to pursue your usual debauchery?"

Kit drew in a deep breath. Once he said it aloud it would be real. There'd be no turning back then. "I came for the season."

Darby had raised his glass, but his hand froze halfway to his lips. "I beg your pardon? Did you say the *season*?"

"I did, yes. I intend to marry, Darby."

"*Marry*?" Poor Darby looked appalled, and despite himself, a grim smile tugged at Kit's lips. Darby was the second son of a wealthy viscount, and like many second sons in London who had nothing much to do aside from amuse themselves, he regarded marriage with the sort of horror usually reserved for things like gentleman's corsets, and the plague.

Kit had been the same, when he'd been a second son.

Alas, he was now a first son. Or rather, the second son

ANNA BRADLEY

of a second son who suddenly found himself, through a brutal process of elimination, the single remaining legitimate Prestwick male, and thus, the Earl of Prestwick.

An earl, God help him, and not just any earl, either, but a *Prestwick* earl. It was a delicate business, being a Prestwick earl, rather more delicate than being any other earl.

"*Marry?*" Darby repeated, staring at him. "Why the devil would you want to do a foolish thing like that?"

What he wanted had nothing to do with it. No, those days were over. It was only fair, perhaps. He'd had twenty-eight years of doing only as he pleased, and now he'd spend the rest of them doing as he must. "I'm the earl now, Darby."

"Yes. What of it? It's not as if any of the other Prestwick earls before you have ever...oh. I see what this is." Darby drained his glass, and slammed it down on the table. "Damn it, Prestwick. This is about that bloody curse, isn't it?"

"No. Not entirely." That is, it was about the curse, yes, but it was also about the title, and the way his Uncle Freddy had died. It was about a dozen things at once, none of which would have been enough to make him mend his wicked ways on their own, but taken together—

"Come now, Prestwick. You don't truly believe all that nonsense about your family's curse, do you?"

Did he? Even now, he wasn't sure. He hadn't used to believe it. He'd been as careless of the alleged curse as every other Earl of Prestwick before him, right up until his Uncle Freddy had met a gruesome end courtesy of a pistol ball to the gut.

4

He'd seen it happen. He'd been Freddy's second, and had witnessed every heartbreaking moment of it as it unfolded. After that...well, it was much easier to dismiss rumors of an ancient curse before his much-beloved uncle and last living relative had expired on a blood-soaked mattress, shrieking in pain.

It had become real to him then, in a way it never had been before.

"But surely you must see how absurd it is, Prestwick. There's no such thing as a curse."

"History says otherwise, Darby. My great-grandfather, my grandfather, my father's elder brother, my father, and now—" He broke off, unable to say Freddy's name.

Darby sighed. "I don't deny it's rather a long list. So you've come to London to choose a countess, because...what? You suppose you can cheat the curse if you marry?"

"Well, I won't cheat it by carrying on as I have been." Every other Earl of Prestwick before him had been an unrepentant scoundrel, only to end up dead in a duel before they'd reached their thirtieth year.

"But *marriage*, Prestwick. That's rather drastic, surely? Can't you just give up one of your mistresses, and stop drinking on Sundays, or something to that effect?"

"Marriage is the least of it, Darby." Every other Earl of Prestwick aside from Uncle Freddy had been married, and it hadn't saved any of them. "The time has come to mend my wicked ways."

"Look, Prestwick. I own there's been, er...rather a run on the Earls of Prestwick." Darby drew his finger across his throat to illustrate his point. "But that

5

doesn't mean the curse isn't nonsense. You realize that, don't you?"

Perhaps it was nonsense. God knew he and Freddy used to laugh about it once upon a time, even as one Prestwick son after another met their ends in a duel.

But this time, it was different. This time, it had happened to Freddy.

And that wasn't all. "There's more, Darby."

Darby must have seen something in his face, because he went still. "What is it? Let's have it all, Prestwick."

"Freddy has a son." Samuel Henry Egan, a tiny bit of a boy, with a downy fuzz of red-gold hair decorating his tiny, two-month old head.

Darby's jaw dropped. "Good Lord. A by-blow?"

"Yes." But still a Prestwick son, if not a future Earl of Prestwick, and an Egan through and through, with that hair. "Before he died, Freddy begged me to take care of him." Freddy's last words had been for Sam, and thank God for it, or else Kit never would have known the boy existed. "Perhaps there isn't a curse, but I'd rather not wager the child's life on it."

"Christ, Prestwick. That's a devil of a thing." Darby was quiet for some time before he drew a breath, and met Kit's eyes. "Very well, then. Have you chosen your future countess?"

"Yes. Lady Harriett Fairmont."

"Fairmont," Darby repeated, his brow furrowing. "Fairmont...what, you mean James Fairmont's younger sister? I believe I met her last winter, when she was in London with her aunt. Timid little mouse of a thing, with dark hair?"

"Yes, that's her. She's in London for the season."

And not a moment too soon. Fate might despise the Prestwick family, but she had thrown a wife right into Kit's path when he most needed one.

"Forgive me, Prestwick, but why Lady Harriett? That is, she's a good choice from a financial perspective. If the gossips have the right of it, she's worth fifty thousand pounds."

"I don't give a damn about her money, Darby." The Prestwick sons might be cursed to die grisly deaths, but they'd always had plenty of money.

"Well, you could do worse, I daresay. She seems to be a sweet young lady, if a bit meek for your tastes."

"For my taste in *mistresses*, yes, but she'll be my wife, Darby." Surely, meekness in a wife was a good thing? "In any case, I didn't choose her. We were promised to each other some time ago."

"Promised, to Lady Harriett?" Darby blinked at him, then rubbed a hand over his eyes. "God above, Prestwick. You're full of secrets, aren't you?"

"It was decided years ago." He and James Fairmont had been good friends once, back when James used to spend his summers in Hampstead Heath with his aunt, Lady Fosberry, who's estate was next door to Prestwick House. "Fairmont and I agreed that if I ever inherited the title, his sister would become the next Countess of Prestwick."

As for Lady Harriett, it had been years since he'd seen her, but he vaguely recalled she'd been a sweet-tempered, agreeable child. With any luck, she'd grown into an agreeable young lady.

"I see. How many years ago was that, Prestwick?"

"Six? Seven, perhaps. What does it matter, Darby?" He'd promised Fairmont he'd marry his sister and make her a countess, and the new Earl of Prestwick wasn't going to be the sort of man who broke his promises. "I said I'd marry her, and I will."

"That's noble of you, but six years is a long time. You can't be certain Fairmont is still in favor of the match."

"What are you saying, Darby? That every fond brother may not wish for his sister to marry a scandalous rake?"

"Er, well—"

"Fairmont is expected to return from the Continent before the end of the season. I've sent a letter to his estate in Hereford, which he'll find upon his return. If he doesn't like the match, I'm certain he'll tell me. God knows what I'll do then. There won't be many young ladies in London eager to settle for a scandalous earl with a curse hanging over his head."

Darby stared at him. "Are you mad, Prestwick? You're an *earl* now, and a wealthy one, at that. You're also under sixty years of age, and in possession of all of your own teeth. You'll have your choice of bride, I assure you."

"Bollocks. No proper young lady wants to marry a rake, Darby."

"You're not a rake any longer, Prestwick. You're an *earl*. The *ton* forgave your past transgressions the instant you inherited the title. I'll be astonished if they don't descend on you like a swarm of locusts the second you set foot in a ballroom."

"I'll be astonished if they do." It was far more likely they'd all scatter like frightened rabbits the moment they laid eyes on him.

"Trust me, Prestwick. You'll soon find yourself the target of every marriage-minded mama in London." Darby rose to his feet and strode to the sideboard.

"They're a crazed lot, especially when it comes to earls. Best prepare yourself."

Kit watched glumly as Darby rummaged through the decanters. "What are you doing?"

"Fetching the brandy, of course." He plucked up a decanter, and then, after a moment's thought, he tucked a bottle of port under his arm. "The port, as well. I've a notion we're going to need them both."

~

"LUCIFER! COME BACK HERE AT ONCE!" Tilly tiptoed past Lady Fosberry's rose arbors, her half boots skidding over the damp ground, cursing herself for a fool with every step.

There was no answer, just some suspicious shuffling coming from a nearby shrub.

"I suppose you think this is all terribly amusing, don't you?" She swatted a branch out of her way with another muttered curse. "Well, it isn't. Not in the least! Do you hear me, Lucifer? You are a *very bad* dog."

Clearly, this wasn't the first time the little demon had tricked one of Lady Fosberry's unsuspecting guests into a midnight romp in the garden. The way he'd whimpered so piteously, and gazed up at her with such sad dark eyes... It had been a performance, from start to finish.

Why, Lucifer put Edmund Kean himself to shame.

The instant she'd set him on the ground, she'd discovered her mistake. Instead of finding a private corner to attend to his business, he'd scampered off, ducking into some thick shrubberies with the glee of the truly wicked.

That had been a half hour ago, and she was still creeping about like a lunatic, trying to coax him back out. "You do realize, Lucifer, that Lady Fosberry will have my head if I lose you? I'll have nothing left but a bloody stump of a neck."

No answer, not even so much as a whine. Lucifer, devil that he was, didn't care about her severed head. God above, who could have guessed such a sweet little dog could be so diabolical? Cats, yes. One could believe it of cats, but weren't dogs meant to be obedient, loyal creatures?

"Lucifer? Come to Tilly, dearest. I've a lovely treat for you, if you'll only come out." It was a lie, of course. Where in the blazes was she meant to find a dog treat at midnight, for pity's sake? The only thing that awaited Lucifer when he reappeared was a hearty scold, but he was a *dog*. There was no way he could know she didn't have a—

"Woof!"

"Lucifer, there you are! Good boy!" A dark nose had emerged from a gap in the branches, and an instant later Lucifer followed, dropping to his bottom in the grass, and gazing up at her with wide, brown doggy eyes.

"That's it, my perfect little angel." She edged closer, preparing to pounce. "Come to Tilly, darling, come to...really, Lucifer, the cut direct? Surely, there's no need for *that*." Though she may as well get used to it, as it was doubtless the first of many she'd receive this season.

Lucifer gave a disdainful sniff, and turned his wet little doggy nose up at her. "Woof!"

"Same to you, you horrid little goblin, er, I mean, that's a good, sweet, lovely little doggy." She crouched low, inching closer, ready to snatch him up at the first opportunity. Close, closer, she nearly had him... "Ah ha! Got you, you menace!"

And she *did* have him, for precisely half a second, but before she had a chance to draw a breath he'd squirmed free, wriggled between the bars of the iron fence that surrounded the garden, and vanished around a corner in a blur of fluffy white fur. "Noooo!"

Why, in the name of all that was just and good, did she always find herself in such absurd scrapes? Because goodness knew charging down the dark streets of Hampstead Heath in her night rail with her unlaced half boots flapping around her ankles certainly qualified as a scrape.

Someone might see her, and then they'd tell Lady Fosberry, and Lady Fosberry would tell Phee, and poor Phee...well, Phee wouldn't scold. She never scolded. No, it would be much worse than that. She'd wouldn't utter a single cross word, but she'd fret herself into a fit over the scandal of it all.

Another scandal, and this one right on the heels of the...er, unfortunate Incident that had taken place just before they'd left for London. There could *not* be another Incident. That was, above all, her first consideration.

Indeed, her very first.

Right after *not* losing Lucius— or Lucifer the Wicked, as she preferred to think of him —Lady Fosberry's precious, beloved dog, who'd run off just now as if he'd had a destination in mind. He was already well ahead of her, and against all reason, his white fur melted seamlessly into the darkness.

She let out a groan and charged after him, her feet sliding about inside her boots, the hem of her night rail dragging behind her. At least she'd had the sense to don her cloak before venturing out, though a cloak wasn't likely to diffuse the scandal that would erupt if anyone happened to see her.

Fortunately, the darkness hid many a wicked deed, and it was as dark as Hades tonight, the moon hiding behind a bank of thick clouds. She could only just make out the hulking presence of Prestwick House looming ahead. It was a pretty place in the daylight, with its rows of airy windows and warm red brick façade, but it appeared rather monstrous tonight, with its shuttered windows and cold chimney stacks. It had stood empty for over a year now, since the last Earl of Prestwick's death, and Lady Fosberry had said she thought it would remain so for some time to come.

The garden gate hadn't been tended to in ages. It was hanging by one hinge, and it let out a high-pitched squeal when she pushed it open, the sound loud enough to wake the dead. She glanced behind her, but Lady Fosberry's house remained still and quiet, the windows dark.

The garden was drowning in shadows. It would be a miracle if she managed to find Lucifer, but she stumbled along in the direction he'd gone, alternating between prayers and curses as she hurried past a long row of tall hedges, peering into the darkness around her for a glimpse of white fur.

But it was no use. There wasn't a strand of fur to be seen, and her heart sank as she wandered from tree to shrub to plants crisp with frost, hissing under her breath with every step. "Lucifer? Do come out, won't you? I beg your pardon for lying about the treat."

Lucifer, alas, wasn't in a forgiving mood. Silence was her only answer, so she crept on, peeking under bushes and rifling through the shrubbery until her hands were covered with long, red scratches from the branches, and her toes were frozen.

A quarter hour passed, then another, and still Lucifer didn't appear. What was the point in going on, under the circumstances? Unless he chose to reveal himself, she had about as much likelihood of finding him as she would a dropped hairpin.

There was nothing for it, but to return to the house, and confess the whole of the debacle to Lady Fosberry, which was sure to be perfectly dreadful. Lucifer was a devious little rascal, but Lady Fosberry quite doted on him. She was going to be horrified when she discovered he'd gone miss—

"Woof!"

"Lucifer?" She jerked toward the sound, her heart jumping into her throat. Oh, please, let it be him! If only she could find him, she'd be ever so careful for the remainder of her time in London. She wouldn't set so much as a single toe out of line—

"Woof!"

"Yes, I'm coming, you beast." She skirted around the corner and darted across a narrow, grassy lane, following the barking until she came to another iron gate. Just beyond it was a small, rather shabby cottage.

She came around the side of it, poking through the underbrush as she went, searching for any sign of Lucifer, but she paused when she reached the entrance of the cottage, blinking.

A narrow shaft of light spilled from the entryway, illuminating the steps beyond.

The front door was cracked open.

An open door, after midnight? How odd.

There didn't seem to be anyone about. Only Lucifer, who was perched on the top step leading up to the door as if he'd done so dozens of times before. Very strange, indeed. So strange, in fact, even a sensible lady like herself might suspect foul play to be involved.

"Woof!" Lucifer was watching her expectantly, as if waiting for her to do something.

"Don't you dare scold me, Lucifer. This is all your fault." Still, Lucifer did have a point. The open door was suspicious, indeed. What if someone inside was ill, or injured? She crept up the stairs, and poked her head through the gap. "Hello? Is there anyone here?"

Silence. The sconces had been lit, but the entryway was deserted.

Lucifer, who'd evidently reached the end of his patience, let out another insistent, "Woof!"

"Hush, you insufferable creature," she hissed, glaring down at him. "If you're so brave, then why don't you go first?"

"Woof!"

"Somehow, I knew you'd say that." She stepped through the door, wincing as the floorboards creaked under her feet, and peeked down the first corridor she came to.

"Woof!"

"I'm *going*, dash it." She crept forward, her heart thumping, afraid every moment someone would leap out at her and demand to know what she was doing, invading their home.

It was dark, as well, but there was a faint glow of lamplight at the end of the hallway. As she drew closer, she could just make out the low murmur of voices.

Oh, thank goodness.

Someone *was* here, they weren't dead, and the last thing she wanted was to be caught sneaking down their hallway. She backed toward the front door, clicking her tongue at Lucifer to follow, but just when she was mere steps from the safety of the garden he shot past her, the click of his toenails against the bare floor deafening in the surrounding silence.

"Lucifer, no!" She hissed, but it was too late. He scampered down the hallway without so much as a backward glance, his fluffy tail wagging madly, and vanished.

CHAPTER
TWO

"Prestwick? Can you hear me? Wake up, man. Is this how you treat your guests?"

Fingers snapped beside Kit's ear, and he unpeeled his eyelids to find an identical pair of dark-haired gentlemen hovering over him, their pale faces swimming before his eyes—

No, wait. There was just one gentleman. It only looked as if there were two. He blinked, but the smirking face continued to weave and bob with such nauseating violence, a flood of bile rushed into his throat. "Darby? Is that you?"

"Of course, it's me. Who else would it be?"

Who, indeed? Whenever he woke with a throbbing head and bloody eyes, Darby tended to be somewhere in the vicinity. "Stay still, will you? You're making me dizzy."

"I rather think that's the fault of the bottle of port you drank."

"Port? Nonsense. I never drank a bottle of port." Kit struggled upright in his chair, outraged, and something slid from under his arm and fell to the floor with a thud. He squinted at it over the arm of the chair.

It was an empty bottle of port. "Or perhaps I did."

"I assure you, you did." Darby collapsed into a nearby chair, falling into an undignified sprawl. "I watched you do it, and I tell you, Prestwick, I've never seen a more disgusting display of drunkenness in my life."

"I find that difficult to believe, unless you don't have any looking glasses in your house."

Darby chortled. "That's the spirit, Prestwick."

Why was his hair so sticky? He rubbed his hand over the matted locks, and his fingers came away streaked with... "Good Lord, is that blood? Am I *bleeding*?"

Darby raised his head from the back of the chair, squinted at Kit, then collapsed back into his sprawl with a shrug. "Only a little. There was a bit of a mishap with some broken glass, I'm afraid. I daresay you'll live."

"That remains to be seen." Kit rubbed a hand over his eyes, blinking, and peered around him. Where the devil was he?

Wherever it was, they had dreadful wallpaper. Good God, were those meant to be cabbage roses? They did look like cabbages, but without a hint of the rose about them. They were rather frightening, really, yet familiar, all the same. He'd certainly seen them before, only he couldn't quite recall...

Oh, yes. He was at the cottage. That was *his* dreadful wallpaper. He was in his own study, and a good thing, as it would save him the trouble of struggling to find his way home.

"Do come here, Fanny," Darby drawled. "It appears Prestwick is alive after all."

Was he? That was a relief, but had Darby said *Fanny*? Because the last bloody thing he wanted right now was—

"My dear Prestwick, I've missed you dreadfully!"

A high-pitched shriek of laughter exploded near his left ear. He slapped his hand over it, turned to Darby and hissed, "What the devil is she doing here?"

"I, ah, I might have mentioned you'd returned to London when I saw her earlier this evening." Darby winced. "I beg your pardon, Prestwick."

"How wonderful that you've come back from the dead, my lord," Fanny cooed. "But I daresay you've been terribly lonely this past twelvemonth. Does he not look lonely, Darby? Do you require some companionship, my lord?"

"God, no. I—*oof!*" Kit stared at the half-dressed lady who'd just landed in his lap. Dark hair, red lips, sleepy eyes, her bosom exposed by the plunging neckline of her gown, which was falling off one shoulder. "Where in God's name did you come from, Fanny?" Had she been clinging to the chandelier above him, and dropped down from the ceiling?

"Don't be tiresome, Prestwick."

Tiresome? No, that wasn't the word for it. He'd arrived in London less than twenty-four hours ago, and already he was exhausted.

"Come now, my lord. I'll take care of you." Fanny wriggled against him and plunged her fingers into his hair, but he jerked away from her touch and lurched to his feet, dumping her into the chair he'd just vacated. She let out an outraged squawk, but he ignored her, and fumbled for his watch.

It was one o'clock in the morning, and judging by the reek of stale air and sweat, and the empty bottles scattered over every surface, he'd been lost in a drunken stupor for some time. Long enough that the half dozen crystal decanters Darby had migrated from the sideboard to the table lay in broken pieces on the floor. "Which one of you devils smashed my crystal?"

Darby yawned. "You did it yourself, Prestwick. You swiped at them with the fireplace poker, and sent the whole lot crashing to the floor."

Kit dragged a hand down his face. He was going to regret asking this— he knew he was. "Why would I smash my own crystal, Darby?"

Darby sighed, as if he were being tiresome, indeed. "You were demonstrating your fencing technique. Don't you remember?"

Fencing, in his study? Good Lord. It wasn't the first time he'd gotten foxed and done something foolish, or even the fiftieth time, but he'd hoped he'd put those days behind him, and was no longer the scoundrel he'd once been.

He *couldn't* be that man. Not anymore.

As for what kind of man he was now...well, that was anyone's bloody guess, but he wasn't going to find the answer at the bottom of a bottle of port. "Right, Darby. It's time for you to depart. Gather your things, and be on your way."

"Yes, do go on, Darby." Fanny waved an imperious hand toward the study door. "Prestwick and I are going to bed, aren't we, darling?"

"I am. You, madam, may do as you please, as long as you do it elsewhere." Kit drew himself up with as much dignity as a man who reeked of port possibly could, and nudged Darby with the toe of his boot. "See to it you take Fanny with you."

Darby let out another long-suffering sigh. "Yes, alright. No need for a tantrum, Prestwick. We're going. Fancy a jaunt to Covent Garden, Fanny?"

"Indeed, I do." Fanny cast Kit a disdainful glance, rose to her feet with an offended flounce of her skirts, and took Darby's arm. "I'm not in the habit of staying where I'm not wanted."

That was debatable, but the promise of more debauchery got them moving quicky enough, and a damned good thing too, as the port Kit had swallowed was gurgling in his belly. It would make a reappearance sooner rather than later, and he'd just as soon cast up his accounts in private.

"Good of you to see us out, Prestwick," Darby drawled as Kit hurried them down the corridor to the entryway, and threw open the front door. "You're quite the gentleman, now you've become an earl."

An earl, yes. A gentleman? Hardly. "Not a bit of it, Darby. I just want to make certain you've gone." The last time Darby had descended on him with a ragged band of villains, he'd nearly broken his neck stumbling over a comatose body at the bottom of his staircase the following morning.

"Dear me, we are cross, aren't we?" Darby gave him an unrepentant grin. "Are you certain you won't accompany us to Covent Garden?"

"As certain as I've ever been of anything in my life." Kit nodded toward the open door of Darby's carriage, and Darby sauntered down the steps, Fanny hanging on his arm.

He handed her in, then turned back to Kit. "About your plans this season, Prestwick. I'm not certain people ever really change, curse or not. Consider carefully before you take on a countess, eh?"

He didn't wait for a reply, but climbed into the carriage after Fanny and signaled his driver to go. Kit ventured onto the stoop and down the steps, watching as the carriage made its way down Heath Street, the rattle of the wheels fading as it turned toward New End Square. Once it was gone, silence descended, and the darkness pressed more closely around him.

He blew out a breath, a stream of frosty air spilling from his lips. At some point during the evening he'd discarded his coat and waistcoat, likely when he'd been displaying his fencing prowess, and the frigid air seeped through the thin layer of his linen shirt, nipping at his collarbones.

He turned and made his way back up the steps, but he paused at the top and peered into the deserted entryway.

Ah, yes.

This was why he needed Darby. He remembered now.

The silence.

But there was nothing for it, but to keep moving forward. He stepped over the threshold, but before he could get through the door a sudden bout of dizziness attacked him, and his legs threatened to buckle under him. He grabbed for the door frame, struggling to right himself, but it was no use. Blood rushed into his head, pounding at his temples and blurring his eyes, and his stomach lurched with nausea.

Once a man was destined to fall, he'd plummet until fate intervened.

So, he gave himself up to it—to the inevitable

tumble backwards, the scuff of his boot heels against the steps, the whoosh of the cold air around him as he fell, and, dimly, the sharp crack of his shoulder against the cobbles as his body met the pavement.

There was no pain, though. A blessing, that.

Just a soft gasp—his own—and then, encroaching darkness.

HE WASN'T GETTING UP AGAIN.

Tilly grasped the iron rails of the fence she'd ducked behind, pushing closer until her chin was in danger of getting wedged in the gap.

Her first night in London, and already she gotten herself into a dreadful mess. It wasn't fair, dash it! She hadn't done a single thing wrong, and here was trouble, already courting her.

She could just return to Lady Fosberry's, and pretend she hadn't seen the open door, or witnessed the man's tumble down the stairs. She could simply go back the way she'd come, and no one would have to know she'd been out here at all.

It wasn't as if she'd done anything wrong. She was perfectly innocent.

But an unconscious man at the bottom of the steps, alone on a frigid night? There was nothing innocent about *that*. She couldn't just leave him here to freeze to death, mere feet from his own front door.

Dash it, this was what came of sneaking about. Phee was going to be furious when she found out about this foray into the garden in the wee, dark hours of the morning— and she *would* find out. She always did, one way or another— but there was no help for it.

Tilly muttered a quick prayer to whatever saint protected young ladies from the consequences of their own foolish choices, and scurried down the garden path toward the man, who hadn't stirred a single inch since he'd fallen down the stairs.

He was splayed out on the ground, his face as pale as death, one side of his forehead smeared with...dear God, was that blood? Had those people who'd just gone bludgeoned him before they took their leave? It hadn't looked like it, but it was so dark. Mightn't they have assaulted him without her seeing it? Had he been burgled, and left for dead?

Oh, Phee was going to be beside herself if she'd managed to stumble upon a murdered gentleman on her very first night in London! She'd get that particular wrinkle between her brows when she found out —the one that belonged to Tilly alone. "Oh, no. No, no, no. Get *up*, damn you."

Alas, he did not get up, but remained sprawled at the foot of the steps.

"Sir? Oh, please, do wake up!" She patted his cheek, but he didn't stir.

Was it possible he was dead? He didn't look dead, precisely, or at least, he didn't look as she'd imagined a dead man ought to look. His eyes were closed, yes, but he looked rather well. He was young, and aside from the blood, quite handsome, with thick, dark eyelashes curled against his flushed cheeks.

She crept closer, her heart in her throat, and knelt down beside him. That was when she smelled it. Port, the sour scent of it so strong about him he must have drunk a great quantity of it.

Either that, or he'd been bathing in it.

He was a drunkard then, but not *dead*, thank goodness. His eyes were closed, but his chest was moving up and down in slow, steady breaths. Quite a chest it was, too. Solid, and thickly-muscled, and he had a pair of correspondingly broad shoulders.

She hadn't a prayer in the world of moving such a large gentleman on her own. "Er, sir?" She nudged one of his shoulders with her finger. "I beg your pardon, but it's time for you to wake up now."

The man didn't appear to agree, because he remained as he was.

Heavens, what a debacle! Perhaps she could just throw a blanket over him, or...no, no. That wouldn't do. She'd have to find someone to help her. Surely, there must be a servant or two lurking inside the house?

"Wait here, sir. I'll be right back." She left him where he was and hurried up his front steps and through the door, but there were no servants lingering in the hallway. "Hello? Is there anyone here? I'm afraid your man here has had a nasty fall."

There was no reply, and the hallway remained deserted. There wasn't a single person, it seemed, who cared if he lived or died. Not one person about to help him, aside from a complete stranger, who shouldn't be here at all.

It was disgraceful. Even if he was a drunkard— which seemed likely, given the amount of port he'd consumed, and his unconscious, bloodied state —he deserved better than this.

What was to be done, then?

She glanced around the entryway, but it was distressingly free of the sort of apparatus required to hoist a large man off the ground.

Unless...

Surely, there must be a study nearby? She tiptoed down the corridor toward a light at the end of the hallway. She wasn't likely to find smelling salts in a man's study, but she'd once roused a kitchen maid who'd fallen into a swoon by sprinkling a little water on her cheeks.

Alas, there wasn't any water to be found in the cramped little room at the end of the hallway. There was a sideboard with a few bottles of spirits arrayed along the top, but no water.

Well then, she didn't have any choice, did she?

She rummaged through the bottles, snatched up one that was half full of pale liquid—sherry, most likely—and marched back outside, the decanter in her hand.

"I'm afraid I really must insist that you wake up at once," she said in her sternest voice, dropping to her knees beside him and shaking his shoulder.

His brow furrowed, and he muttered something, but his eyes remained closed.

"You can't stay here. You'll freeze to death. Surely, you don't want that?"

She shook his shoulder again, and this time he made a clumsy effort to push her away, but she evaded him easily. "Now, none of that, if you please. I'm trying to help you."

"...told you to go, Fanny."

Fanny? Who was Fanny? His lover? How titillating.

But this was hardly the time to delve deeper into the man's scandals, particularly if she didn't wish to

26

become one of them, which she certainly would, if she lingered here any longer.

It would have to be the sherry, then.

It took a bit of tugging to remove the stopper, but she managed it. She leaned over him, and tipped the bottle toward his mouth. A few stray drops escaped, and splashed onto the white linen of his shirt.

Oh, dear. That didn't look like sherry. It was *green*. Not a lurid, poisonous green, thank goodness, but a pale, harmless-looking green. Still, green spirits? Surely, it wasn't wise to toss green spirits into people's faces?

She jerked the bottle back, but the liquid—whatever it was—rushed from the mouth, and splashed directly into the man's face.

"Arggh!" He jerked as if he'd been struck, his hands flying to his face. "What the *devil*?"

Oh, no. She hadn't meant to douse him quite so thoroughly. "I do beg your pardon—"

"For God's sake, Fanny!"

Whoever this Fanny was, Tilly didn't envy her in the least. But at least he was alive, if a bit confused. "I'm not—"

"You nearly drowned me in absinthe!" He rolled over onto his side, coughing and spluttering. "It's burning my eyes!"

Absinthe? Oh, no. Of all the bottles on the sideboard, why had fate led her to *that* one? Wasn't absinthe meant to drive people mad? Perhaps she'd better be on her way, before he returned to his senses, and began asking questions she'd rather not answer.

Her name, for instance.

She scrambled to her feet, and began to inch

backward, away from him. "Er, it was an accident. I didn't mean to..."

But what could she say? There was no explanation that would do, no scenario in which sneaking about a man's house at night and throwing absinthe in his face could possibly be made to sound innocent.

So, she did what any young lady who didn't choose to be embroiled in a scandal *would* do in such circumstances.

Turned, and ran. Alas, she didn't get far.

A large hand snaked out, grabbed the hem of her cloak and jerked her to a halt. "Oh no, you don't." Long, strong fingers wrapped tightly around her ankle, holding her fast. "You're not going anywhere."

CHAPTER
THREE

"Release me this instant!" She kicked at him, her heel coming dangerously close to striking his forehead, but he had a tight grip on her ankle, which was impressive given he'd just narrowly escaped being drowned in a flood of absinthe.

Drowned, and blinded. The spirits burned like acid, scalding his eyeballs with such fiery intensity he couldn't bear to open his eyes. It was pure luck he'd managed to grab hold of her at all.

But now he had her, he wasn't letting her go.

"Get off!" She squirmed and clawed against his hold, flopping about like an outraged fish at the end of a hook. "For pity's sake, I was only trying to help you!"

Help him? "By dousing me with absinthe?"

"I didn't...I thought it was sherry!"

Was that meant to reassure him? "I prefer my spirits be served in a tumbler, not dashed in my face!"

Looming above him was a blurry madwoman, and she was...good Lord, was she holding one of his heavy crystal decanters in her hand? It was a wonder she hadn't bludgeoned him to death!

29

She still might, come to that. He tightened his fingers around her ankle and tugged, hoping to topple her to the ground before she could crack his skull in two. "Put the decanter down, before you do something you'll regret!"

She didn't answer, but the decanter slipped from her hand and dropped to the ground in an explosion of glass. She fell to her knees beside him and began clawing at his hands in a desperate attempt to get free. "Let go of my ankle, sir, or I'll be forced to take drastic measures!"

More drastic than strangling? Because somehow, with all their tussling the neck of his shirt had tightened into a noose, and was pressing into his windpipe. "Stop thrashing about, would you? We're not getting anywhere like this. Be still, and I'll release you, and I vow on my honor as a gentleman I won't harm you."

It wasn't much of a vow, considering he wasn't a gentleman.

But shockingly, she did as he bid her. Her hands fell away, and he rolled onto his back, the absinth running in sticky rivulets down his neck. He shook his head to clear it, droplets of sticky absinthe flying from the ends of his hair in every direction, until at last he caught his breath.

He squinted down at her, but he was still coughing and spluttering from the foul liquid that had found its way up his nose. He couldn't see a bloody thing, aside from a vaguely female-shaped person with a cloud of dark hair. "Is that you, Fanny? I told you before I left London, we're finished. Attacking me is hardly the way to try and wriggle yourself back into my good graces."

A brief, stunned silence fell, followed by a most unladylike snort. "My, you *do* think highly of yourself, if you believe a lady would attack you merely because you deprived her of your company."

"Yet here you are."

"Oh, for pity's sake." There was a heavy sigh. "I'm not Fanny, as you'd find out for yourself if you'd open your eyes."

"I'd like to, but unfortunately, they're sealed shut with absinthe."

"Shall I fetch the sherry, then? Perhaps it would help unstick them."

Her voice was low, a bit husky, and entirely unlike Fanny's shrill tones. His eyes were streaming, but he struggled upright, pried his eyelids apart, and studied the indistinct face swimming before him.

Dark hair, brown eyes, a heart-shaped face, and a pair of pink lips that hinted at a delicious plumpness, even as they were flattened in a frown.

He blinked, then blinked again. She was quite right.

She *wasn't* Fanny. He'd never laid eyes on this lady before. "Who the *devil* are you?"

"No one. That is, we're, er...not acquainted with each other."

"No? Are you in the habit, madam, of sneaking about stranger's private gardens, and attempting to murder gentlemen you aren't acquainted with, then? Are you some sort of female villain?"

"I wasn't sneaking! I was, er, looking for something."

"In my garden? What could you possibly be looking—"

"And if I had wanted to murder you, I might have

done so easily, because you left your front door open to whatever scoundrel chose to stroll through it."

"Open?" Had he neglected to close the cottage door when Darby arrived? Damn it, he couldn't remember. The entire evening was a blur. "I don't...that doesn't make any sense."

"Not much, no." She let out another sigh, scrambled up onto her knees beside him, and peered down into his face. "You don't look at all well. We'd better get you up."

Yes, that was a good idea. He flailed about for a bit, but his limbs didn't appear to be working properly, and he fell back with a grunt.

She reached for him, and gave his shirt a determined tug, only to topple back over onto her backside. "Goodness, you're heavy! A bit of help, if you can manage it?"

"I'm not in the habit of assisting my attackers, madam." Yet he struggled onto his knees anyway, as it wouldn't do to lounge about while there was a murderess in his garden.

That turned out to be a mistake, however, because as soon as he was upright, dizziness swamped him. His head felt as if it had met the sharp end of a fireplace poker. "God above. What did you hit me with?"

"Me?" She blinked innocently at him, a pair of long lashes falling over her dark eyes. "I never hit you."

"Well, someone bloody did." It hurt like the devil, too. He reached up to assess the damage, wincing. His hair was sticky, and his hand came away red with blood.

"Doubtless, they did." She shrugged, as it made

perfect sense to her that someone would want to bludgeon him. "Either that, or you fell down the stairs and struck your head on the ground. Don't you remember anything?"

He rested his back against the step behind him, and lifted the edge of his shirt to his nose, taking a cautious sniff. No, he hadn't imagined the absinthe. "I remember you dousing me with absinthe."

She bit her lip. "Yes, that was, ah, perhaps not the best solution. As I said, I thought it was sherry. I did try to rouse you, but you refused to wake, and I had to do something. I couldn't just leave you here."

"You have no knowledge of how I happened to end up here?" The answer was hovering just on the edge of his consciousness, but he couldn't quite reach it.

"It's hardly a mystery." She sniffed. "Alas, the truth is nowhere near as exciting as a female villain come to murder you. That would have been a much better story than your drinking too much port, falling down the stairs and hitting your head."

Port? No, he hadn't...oh, wait. Yes, he had. It all came flooding back to him, then.

He'd followed Darby and Fanny to the door, but he'd been struck by a bout of dizziness before he could get back inside. Pathetic, really, and uncomfortably reminiscent of the man he'd been when he'd last been in London.

Had it really only been a single year? He'd been happy enough to spend every night in a drunken stupor before Freddy's death, but with one shot from a pistol, everything had changed.

It seemed as if he'd lived a dozen lives since then.

One day. He'd been back in London for *one day*,

and he'd already broken the only promise he'd made to himself. A single day, and it looked as if he'd have done much better to remain in the country.

Perhaps Darby was right— perhaps people didn't change, and this was all a waste of time. But the season was underway, and his promised bride awaited. If history had taught him nothing else, it had proven beyond any doubt that Fate didn't look kindly upon Earls of Prestwick who lived lives of shameless debauchery.

God, poor Freddy—

"You're a bit bloody, I'm afraid. I think we'd better get you inside." She clambered to her feet, and held her hand out to him. "Here, take my hand, and I'll help you up."

"How do you propose to do that?" His vision had cleared, and though she was still lost in shadows, he could see well enough to discern a slight, slender figure. "You're too small to support me. I'll send us both sprawling."

"Nonsense. I'm much sturdier than I look."

He didn't like it, but he'd pensioned off all the servants after Freddy had been... well, *after*— and he'd sent his valet to bed hours ago. Unless he fancied spending the night in the garden, he'd have to accept her assistance.

"Alright." He caught her hand— a worryingly small, dainty hand —taking care to bear as much of his own weight as he could manage, but his legs weren't quite steady. She staggered a bit before she got her balance, but slowly they made their way up the steps.

He stopped when they reached the top. "Perhaps

you'd better let me go now, and go back to..." Wherever it was she'd come from.

"No, indeed. You're staggering as it is. If I let go, you'll only fall down the stairs again. Stop fussing, for pity's sake, and let me help you inside."

Overbearing chit. Still, he didn't fancy another tumble, and he didn't trust himself to remain upright. He clung to the railing as they shuffled up the stairs, one slow, cautious step at a time, both of them panting when they reached the top.

"Which way is it?"

He glanced down at his companion— or was she his savior? He hadn't quite made up his mind what to make of her—who was sagging under his weight, and making a valiant attempt to hide it.

It didn't seem wise to tempt fate by a journey up the long, curving staircase to his bedchamber on the second floor, so he nodded toward the corridor on the right. "My study. It's the last door on the right."

She drew in a breath, straightening her shoulders, and together they hobbled from the entryway down the corridor to his study. The door stood open, and she led him to a settee on one side of the fireplace. The fire was still burning in the grate, and a good bloody thing, too, as his shirt was wet, and clinging damply to his chest.

Once they were there, she wasted no time in dumping him unceremoniously onto the settee. "This settee looks dreadfully uncomfortable, but it's better than the floor. My goodness, where did all this broken glass come from?"

Oh yes, he'd forgotten. His study floor was an ocean of shattered crystal. "Apparently there was, ah...a bit of a fencing bout earlier in the evening."

"Fencing?" Her eyebrows rose. "In your *study*?"

"So I'm told, yes." He thrust a pillow under his head, swung his feet up and lay back, stretching out on the settee.

Without any self-consciousness whatsoever, she plopped down into the chair across from him and fixed those dark eyes on him with an interest she didn't bother to hide. "Your head is still bleeding. Shall I ring for a servant to see to it?"

"That's not necessary." He wasn't going to wake his valet. It wasn't poor Cheever's fault he'd made his way to the bottom of a bottle of port, and taken a tumble down the stairs.

She sighed, then took up the cravat he'd abandoned earlier in the evening. "Here. Perhaps this will help." She knelt on the floor beside the settee, and pressed it to the stinging cut on his temple. "Do you suppose you've concussed yourself?"

"I don't think so, no." He closed his eyes, fell back against the pillow, and gave himself up to the gentle pressure of her fingers, the soft brush of her fingertips in his hair. After a little while the throbbing in his head receded a bit, and he opened his eyes, taking in the face hovering beside him.

She was young, not more than nineteen or twenty years old, with a sharp little chin, full pink lips, a tumble of wild chestnut hair, and a pair of blue eyes with a thick fringe of dark eyelashes. Blue eyes, not brown, as he'd first thought. Not an ordinary blue, either, but a blue so dark in the dim light they were nearly sapphire.

Where in the world had she come from? He glanced at the mantel clock. It was close to two o'clock in the morning. What sort of young lady wandered about alone in the dark?

Only one kind. But what was she doing *here*? This was Hampstead Heath, not Covent Garden.

Unless...had Darby sent him a doxy? It was the sort of thing Darby would do, and God knew there was no other rational explanation for the girl's presence here.

She was alluring, and temptingly close. So very close, her breath warm against his lips, her fingers caressing his heated skin until the ache in his head gave way to a heavier, deeper ache in his groin.

It had been a long time for him— endless, lonely days in Ashford, the silence so relentless it became a roaring in his head, a weight holding him down, flattening him into nothingness, and it was here too, that terrible silence, lying in wait to devour him again...

He caught her wrist in his hand, and drew her closer.

She stared at him, her eyes wide, and a deep, fathomless blue. "What are you..."

Her words trailed off as he took her chin in his fingers and tilted her face up to his. "Kissing you," he whispered, just before he took her lips. She froze against him, her body going stiff, but as he teased her lips open and delved inside she melted into him, gasping softly as he took her mouth deeply, tasting her.

She was so sweet, the deep, mossy scent of the garden clinging to her skin, and dear God, he couldn't get enough of her. He slid his hands down to her waist, taking her mouth deeply as he urged her more tightly against him, and it felt like drowning, kissing her, like being swept up in a warm wave of desire, every inch of his body straining for her—

"Stop!" A pair of small hands landed on his chest and shoved him back, hard, then she leapt to her feet, her trembling fingers pressed to her mouth. "What do you think you're doing?"

"I was..." Well, it was obvious, wasn't it? At least, it would have been so to a doxy.

Except now the fog of desire had begun to clear, he could plainly see she didn't *look* like a doxy. She looked like an innocent, with those sweet pink lips, and her reaction...she was the very picture of out-raged virtue. "I, ah, I beg your pardon. I thought you were a—"

He stopped himself just in time, but she heard it as clearly as if he'd said the word aloud. "How *dare* you? Why, I should have left you outdoors to freeze!"

Damned if he wasn't beginning to wish the same. "I take it Darby didn't send you here to, er...entertain me this evening, then?"

"I don't know any Darby, and I assure you, no amount of money could induce me to stay the night with you!"

"If Darby didn't send you, then how did you happen to make your way into my garden tonight?" Innocents didn't wander about alone at night, for God's sake. None of this made any sense!

"Not in the way *you* imagine." She crossed her arms over her chest, glaring at him. "I was—" She broke off, her eyes going wide. "Lucifer!"

"I beg your pardon?" He was no angel, certainly, but surely that was a bit of an exaggeration. "There's no need for name calling."

"Not *you*, the dog!"

Dog? What bloody dog? Had she lost her mind? "There's no—"

But in the next instant, there *was* a dog. At least *something* with fluffy white fur had just pranced into the middle of the room. "How the devil did he get into my study?"

"I told you, your front door was open. He darted inside." She didn't spare him a glance, but crept toward the dog, who'd plopped himself down in the center of the carpet as if he'd done so dozens of times before. "Lucifer? Come here, sweetheart."

The dog let out a petulant whine, watching her warily.

"Come here, Lucifer, or I promise you, you'll regret—yes, that's it, darling. Such a good boy..." She swooped down, snatched up the dog, and straightened with a squirming ball of fur in her arms. "Ah, ha! Got you, you devil."

He stared at the dog, something tugging at his memory. "I've seen that dog before."

Her eyes went wide. "Oh, no, I'm sure you're confused. It's the head injury, no doubt." She edged toward the study door, the dog clutched in her arms. "I wish you the best of luck in recovering your wits, such as they are. Goodbye!"

"Wait! What's your name, and how did you happen to be—"

But it was too late.

She'd already disappeared through his study door, her white muslin skirts flying out behind her. Only they didn't look like skirts, with that narrow band of lace at the hems. They looked like...

God above, was she wearing a night rail?

He staggered to his feet, wincing at the burst of

pain in his head, and stumbled after her, but just as he reached the corridor, she fled through the front door.

He staggered after her, through the entryway and onto the steps, but her dark, slender shadow had already skirted the edge of the iron fence surrounding the cottage garden. She darted past the shrubberies to the pathway beyond, and turned...

Straight into Lady Fosberry's rose garden.

The faint squeal of the garden gate echoed in the still, dark night, and then silence descended again. A few moments later, a candle flickered in one of the bedchambers on the third floor of Fosberry House.

He stared up at the dancing light, his stomach lurching.

The girl was no doxy. She was a guest of Lady Fosberry's, likely the daughter or niece of some viscount or earl or other, here for the season.

She was a *lady*, with a reputation to lose, and she'd been in his house, with *him*.

At night. Alone.

In her night rail.

And he'd *kissed* her. Not an innocent brush of his lips against her knuckles, or a chaste kiss on her forehead, but a deep, wet, drugging kiss. He'd tasted her lips, her tongue.

He'd been in London for a single night, and he'd already compromised an innocent.

A shiver gripped him, the icy air wrapping around his bare throat like a fist.

The Prestwick curse had found him.

CHAPTER
FOUR

N one of the devout souls crowded into the pews of St. George's this morning could accuse Tilly of anything less than the strictest piety.

She'd worn her most demure gown—a white cambric monstrosity with a stiff, frilled collar at the throat, and a dull green robe with fussy cambric trimmings. She'd even included a white mob cap under her straw bonnet, lest any wayward locks of her hair chose to stage one of their frequent mutinies.

The mob cap had been a mistake. The wretched thing itched as if dozens of spiders were crawling over her scalp, but one would never know it to look at her. She'd borne the torment without squirming. Indeed, she hadn't stirred a single inch since she'd taken her seat, not even when her neck began to ache from being bent so long over her prayer book, and her backside had gone numb from the hard wooden pew assaulting it.

It was all most unpleasant, but it was essential she present such a flawless picture of female virtuousness, no one would ever suspect the truth.

She hadn't come to church this morning to hear the sermon.

No, she'd come to *spy*.

This was London, after all. *Mayfair*, no less, and St. George's was the most fashionable church in the city. It was always stuffed to the rafters with the most fashionable *ton*, but particularly so today, as it was the last Sunday before the start of the season.

She might reasonably expect to catch sight of a notorious rake or two, or at the very least, a merry widow or demi-rep. She did want a quick peek at one, just to satisfy her curiosity.

But she hadn't come to London to gawk at the rakes. No, she was searching for someone else entirely. If the handsome, the charming, the inimitable Earl of Wyle really was in town to search for a countess, as rumor claimed, she wanted to get a look at him before the season commenced.

Not for herself, of course, but for Harriett.

Alas, even if such a fascinating personage as Lord Wyle were here, *she* couldn't see him, hemmed in as she was next to Harriett, with Lady Fosberry on one side of them, and Phee on the other. She was wedged into the pew tighter than a pea in an excessively narrow pod.

Not by accident, either. Phee would never be so unkind as to say so, but Tilly suspected her sister had herded her into this position, in the same way a shepherd might herd a naughty sheep.

Perhaps it was for the best. Goodness knew a young lady could hardly stir a step in wicked old London without tumbling into a scandal. Why, even an innocent stroll in the garden could lead to disaster. Only *here* could a pure act of charity on the part of a blameless young lady turn into a shocking kiss in the blink of an eye.

If anyone had had happened to see her last night—

But they *hadn't*, and the less she dwelled on past mistakes, the better. She was in London now, and determined not to put a single toe out of line. There would be no scrapes, scandals, mishaps or childish antics. Phee's brow would remain smooth, because Tilly would be behave as a proper young lady should from the start of the season to the end.

For the most part, that is. Spying wasn't ladylike, but she was doing it for Harriett's sake and not her own, so it didn't count, did it?

Harriett, much like every other young lady in London for the season was enamored of Lord Wyle. One might hope his lordship would prove to be discriminating enough to separate the wheat from the chaff, but it wouldn't hurt to get a peek at him before the stampede began.

Thankfully, one didn't need to move in order to spy. She'd done it often enough at home, though it must be said the parishioners in Hambleden didn't provide her with much diversion. The only scandalous event that ever took place at St. Mary's was poor old Mrs. Apsley dozing through the Lord's Prayer, her snoring breaths stirring the feathers in her hat into a frenzy.

But this was subtle spying. *Ladylike* spying.

There would be no gawking. Nothing as untoward as that. Not with every eye in the church upon them. Not that she could blame the good parishioners of St. George's for gaping at them. It wasn't every day two of the infamous Templeton sisters traipsed down the center aisle of St. George's in the first week of the London season.

Now, if all five of them had been here, well...one shuddered to think of the furor such an excess of Templetons would cause among the *ton*, but Phee, with her usual presence of mind, had insisted that Emmeline, Juliet and Helena forego Tilly's season, and remain in the country.

Still, it was bad enough, even without all of her sisters here.

Poor Phee. She must be ready to crawl underneath the pew by now. Indeed, nothing less than a season for Tilly could have persuaded Phee to come to London at all, but she needn't have worried, because there would be no scandals. Not this time.

Not a single whisper, a hint of gossip, or a breath of rumor would find them *this* time.

This time, she was in perfect control of herself.

Still, a season. She stifled a sigh. A *season*, of all absurd things. Rather a waste of time and effort, given she had no intention of marrying. Why, she'd sooner stand on her head in the middle of Mayfair and recite lines from Byron's most salacious poems than accept a gentleman's hand.

Marriage was all perfectly well for some young ladies, but she'd never fancied it. Gentlemen were wearying creatures, and now that three of her older sisters had gone off and married earls, their family was no longer in dire financial straits.

Thus, there was no reason for *her* to marry at all. Which was fortunate, as she hadn't a prayer of attracting a proper gentleman, and wouldn't know what to do with him if she did.

So, she might do as she pleased, and if she didn't

relish a lifetime in the small, dull village of Ham-bleden with nothing more exciting to do than listen to Mrs. Aspley's snores, she relished leaving Phee there alone even less.

No, that simply wouldn't do. She'd *never* abandon Phee.

All she had to do was get through the season without becoming betrothed, and without causing even the faintest whiff of scandal that might hurt or embarrass Phee. As a reward, she'd have the pleasure of watching Harriett, who was the sweetest, dearest friend a young lady could ask for, capture the heart of her chosen gentleman.

Although it must be said that her spying wasn't going as well as she'd hoped. Either Lord Wyle hadn't attended church this morning, or he was tucked into some far corner outside the range of her roving gaze.

She'd never before laid eyes on the man, but Har-riett had insisted they couldn't possibly miss him, as he was a head taller than every other gentleman, and boasted an impressive quantity of thick, golden hair Harriett swore was as sleek and soft-looking as the finest cornsilk. Why any young lady would want a gentleman with cornsilk hair Tilly couldn't say, but then she wasn't the starry-eyed romantic Harriett was—

"Ahem." Beside her, Harriett delicately cleared her throat.

Tilly cast a sidelong glance at her friend. Harri-ett's head was bent virtuously over her prayer book, but one of her gloved fingers was raised, and pointing to the left.

Tilly glanced up over the edge of her bonnet's brim. She had a clear view of the rows of pews above

45

them, all of them crowded with fashionably-attired aristocrats. "Where?" She kept her voice low, the words more breath than sound.

"Left corner." Harriet spoke from the corner of her mouth, her lips hardly moving. "Behind the lady with the enormous ostrich feather."

Ah, yes. There was no hope of seeing his face with that blasted feather in the way, but she caught a glimpse of a golden head, and half of a broad shoulder. If they could secure an introduction to him today, he'd almost certainly invite Harriett to dance at Lady Fosberry's ball on Tuesday.

"After church," she whispered. "Be ready."

Harriett said nothing, but she reached across her prayer book, and curled her pinky around Tilly's.

~

"MY GOODNESS, Tilly! Must you charge across the churchyard like a horse out of the gate?" Phee caught her arm and tugged Tilly back to her side. "What has you in such a hurry?"

"Nothing. Nothing at all, I just, er..." Tilly cast a surreptitious look at Harriett. Alas, Harriett wasn't as practiced at intrigue as one might wish, and only gave her a wide-eyed look in return. "It's just that London is so exciting, is it not? There are so many fashionable people!"

Phee frowned. "Fashionable? Since when have you ever cared one whit about fashion? You've always claimed it's the dullest thing imaginable."

She *didn't* care about fashions, but really, it was excessively tedious of Phee to always be so observant. "Since I came to London, of course. There's not much point in being interested in fashions in Hambleden, is there?"

Phee didn't look convinced, but Lady Fosberry gave an indulgent laugh. "Just so, Tilly. One must be terribly elegant at St. George's of a Sunday, or suffer the scorn of the *ton*."

"Which gentleman do you think the most fashionable, Harriett?" Tilly gave Harriett a nudge. If they were going to secure an introduction to Lord Wyle before the first ball of the season, this was their best chance.

"Oh! Everyone is terribly elegant, are they not?" Harriett hesitated, a pretty pink flush flooding her cheeks as she cast a shy glance toward Lord Wyle. "But that gentleman, just there, in the navy frock coat, with the striped waistcoat looks particularly well."

At least half a dozen gentleman within shouting distance were wearing navy frock coats and striped waistcoats, but by some magical powers of deduction, Lady Fosberry knew precisely which gentleman Harriett was referring to.

"My dear Harriett, you could hardly have chosen better. That gentleman is Lord Wyle, and he's the pinnacle of elegance. Every young lady in London this season has set her heart on him." Lady Fosberry took Harriett's arm. "Come along, and I'll introduce you to him."

Tilly linked her arm with Phee's and went to hurry after them, but Phee, who had little use for gentlemen, particularly fashionable ones, held back. "We can't just accost the man."

"Don't be silly. We're not going to accost him, only..." She trailed off, her eye catching on a knot of young gentlemen gathered near the front entrance of the church.

Phee was right— she wasn't interested in fashions, and even less interested in fashionable gentlemen, especially peacocks like these, but they *were* extraordinarily pretty, and it wasn't in her nature—or indeed, any young lady's nature—to ignore a crowd of pretty gentlemen.

They were all dressed in the latest fashions, but one gentleman stood out from the rest. He was a head taller than the others surrounding him, and wore a flawlessly tailored olive green coat that accentuated his muscular shoulders, and a pair of tight-fitting cream-colored pantaloons that accentuated his...well, nothing a proper young lady should take notice of, that was certain.

He was dressed just as a young gentleman should be, without the extravagant embroidered silk and fussy laces some gentlemen affected, and he had the loveliest auburn hair as well, the ends of the thick, wavy locks just visible under the brim of his black silk top hat. It was an unusual dark russet shade, highlighted with plentiful strands of the most charming red gold, rather like...

Oh. Oh, *no*. Dear God.

It couldn't be, could it? Surely, she'd made a mistake?

But no. It *could* be him. It *was* him. There was no mistake. If the breadth of his shoulders hadn't given him away, then the straight, aristocratic nose and angular jaw certainly did.

The drunkard, the rake, the scoundrel from last night who'd accused her of being a prostitute was standing on the corner of St. George and Maddox

Streets, fresh from his Sunday prayers, looking like an auburn-haired angel in his smart olive green coat.

God above, who was he? A gentleman, certainly, or rather, a wicked rake with the *appearance* of a gentleman. But when had that ever made a difference to the *ton*?

Whatever—or whoever—he was, he mustn't see her. "Would you mind terribly if we returned to the carriage, Phee? I've a sudden headache."

"Oh, dear. You do look a bit pale." Phee took her arm and hurried her toward the carriage. Fortunately, Lady Fosberry's driver was nearby, and they made it through the throng and into the safety of the carriage without attracting any attention.

Tilly breathed out a sigh of relief as she tucked herself into the corner of the seat, taking care to keep her face away from the window. Dear God, that had been a near thing! Why, they'd been less than two paces from him. It was a miracle he hadn't seen her. If they'd tarried even a moment longer in the churchyard, he certainly would have, and then what?

Scandal, that's what, and what a delicious one it would be. The youngest of the infamous Templeton sisters, cavorting with a drunken gentleman at *night*, in a deserted cottage, not a single day after she'd arrived in London!

That wasn't what had happened, of course, but that's how the gossips would tell it. Once again, the Templetons would be humiliated, and Phee's heart... oh, Phee's poor, fragile heart would be broken.

Oh, *why* hadn't she left him where he'd fallen last night? Whoever had said a good deed never went unpunished had the right of it!

"Well, my dears, that was a triumph!" Lady Fosberry announced when she and Harriett returned to the carriage. "Lord Wyle was quite taken with Harriett. He's attending my ball on Tuesday evening, of course, and he insisted she save him a dance. You must write to James, Harriett, and tell him of your success!"

Harriett's cheeks went pink. "I will, Aunt, though I'm sure Lord Wyle would have asked the same of any young lady."

"Nonsense. He admired you, child. I can always tell."

Harriett flushed up to the roots of her hair. "I suppose we'll see, won't we?" She said no more, but turned to gaze out the window, a dreamy smile on her lips.

Tilly glanced over Harriett's shoulder. The knot of young gentlemen had moved to the corner of St. George's Street, where the carriages slowed just before making the turn onto Maddox Street. There, so close she could touch him if she thrust her hand out the window, was the mysterious, auburn-haired gentleman.

Who was he? She had to know, *now*.

She cast a furtive glance at Phee, but she was lost in her own thoughts, her gaze on her hands in her lap, and Harriett was similarly occupied with her daydreams of Lord Wyle.

Neither of them were paying any attention to Tilly.

Their carriage was next in the queue to make the turn. In another moment, she'd lose sight of the man. This was her best chance, and she'd be a fool not to seize it. So, she leaned close to Lady Fosberry, and whispered, "Who is that gentleman, just there on the corner?"

Lady Fosberry peered out the window. "Which gentleman? There are half a dozen of them."

"The one with the auburn hair, in the olive green coat."

"Where? I don't see—" Lady Fosberry broke off with a soft gasp. "My goodness. I didn't expect to see *him* in London this season."

The carriage turned then, and Tilly was obliged to crane her neck to get a last glimpse of the gentleman as they made their way down Maddox Street. "Who? Who is he?"

"My dear girl, *that* is Christopher Egan."

Egan, Egan...where had she heard that name before?

"The Earl of Prestwick," Lady Fosberry added.

"*That's* the Earl of Prestwick?" Tilly fell back against the seat, her stomach quivering like a jelly.

"He is, indeed, since his uncle died unexpectedly last year. A duel, you know. Rather a tragedy, as he was quite young, but then the Prestwick gentlemen do tend to expire before their time." Lady Fosberry gave her a sly smile. "Do you think him handsome, Mathilda?"

What a question! Or could it even be called a question at all, when there was only one conceivable answer? Whatever else Lord Prestwick might be— rake, scoundrel, drunkard—he was undeniably handsome.

But then, beauty and wickedness often went hand in hand, and it seemed that was never more true than with Lord Prestwick. "It hardly matters what I think.

But didn't you say he wouldn't be in London this season?"

"I didn't think he would be. Indeed, it's entirely out of character. Now he's here, I must remember to send him an invitation to my ball."

"The ball?" Dear God, that dreadful incident in the garden was quickly becoming the stuff of nightmares. "But *why* must you?"

"Oh, our families have known each other for years. Kit—the Earl of Prestwick, I mean, but he's always been Kit to me—was great friends with my nephew James when they were younger. I'm tremendously fond of him. He was a kind, decent boy, but like every Prestwick before him, he turned wicked."

Oh, so very wicked! Not a single rogue in London could hold a candle to the Earl of Prestwick.

"I can't imagine what he's doing here, unless he..." Lady Fosberry trailed off, her brow puckering.

"Unless?"

"Hmm? Oh, nothing, dear. Nothing at all."

It didn't look like nothing. It looked like *something*.

"I wonder..." Lady Fosberry began, but once again, she trailed off.

"What? What do you wonder?"

"Hmm?" Lady Fosberry startled, as if she'd forgotten Tilly was there. "Oh, nothing, dear. Nothing at all."

CHAPTER

FIVE

"I don't know if I can do this, Tilly." Harriett stared at her reflection in the looking-glass, her chin wobbling. "My stomach is all aflutter."

"Thank you, Maria," Tilly murmured to the lady's maid who'd been helping her and Harriett prepare for the ball. "You may go."

"Yes, Miss Mathilda." Maria fastened the last of the tiny buttons marching in a row down Harriett's back, dipped into a curtsey, and quietly withdrew.

Tilly waited until the bedchamber door had closed behind Maria before she turned to Harriett. "Of course you can, dearest. Why, a ball is the simplest thing in the world!" Simply monstrous, in truth, but she couldn't say so to Harriett, who looked like a panicked horse about to bolt.

"But what if I can't?" Harriett's dark eyes were shiny with unshed tears. "What if no one asks me to dance?"

"My dearest Harriett, this ball is being held in *your* honor. Your aunt will make certain you're partnered for every dance, though I daresay there will be no need for her to intervene, as the gentlemen will all be clamoring for your hand tonight."

Harriett sniffed. "Do you really think so?"

"Of course, I do. Why shouldn't they? You look lovely."

"So you do, Tilly." Harriett gave her a watery smile. "I adore your gown. It flatters you."

"It better do." Tilly tugged at the tight silk bodice of her gown. "Because it's clearly going to be a torment to wear."

But Harriett wasn't looking at her. She was staring at her own reflection, her lips turned down.

"Harriett?" Tilly crossed the room. "Is something amiss with your gown?"

Harriett met her gaze in the glass, forced a smile, and gave a little shake of her head. "No, nothing at all. I'm being silly. It's just that this is our first ball of the season, and I'd hoped... well, never mind. It doesn't matter."

It *did* matter, because Harriett's lips had gotten all trembly again. "It is your gown, isn't it? Do you not care for it?"

"It's very pretty, and I liked it well enough at the modistes', but now I'm not sure it suits me. And my hair, Tilly." Harriett raised a hand to her head and ran her fingertips over the stiff curls pinned beside her ears. "It's not quite the thing, is it?"

It *was* the thing. A number of young ladies were wearing their hair in clusters of elaborate curls at their temples this season. The trouble was, it wasn't the thing for *Harriett*.

"Never mind it, Tilly. I won't be so selfish as to complain, and hurt my aunt's feelings." Harriett turned away from the glass, and gave Tilly a brave smile. "Shall we go downstairs?"

"There's nothing selfish about wishing to look your best for your first ball of the season, Harriett." She took Harriett by the shoulders and turned her back toward the glass. "It's not the gown's color. This shade of blue is lovely on you. The trouble is the trimmings. Why, you're positively drowning in bows and ribbons, and this hairstyle is too fussy."

"Well, I don't see what we can do about it now. It's too late to change it." Harriett let out a forlorn little sigh. "My aunt and Euphemia are likely already wondering what's become of us."

"They may wait a few more minutes." She couldn't let her friend appear at her first ball looking anything less than breathtaking. Harriett was as lovely as any other young lady in London this season. Unfortunately, the only person who couldn't see that was Harriett herself.

She turned a critical eye on Harriett's gown, fingered the bows at the waist and neckline of the bodice, then gave a decisive nod. "I know just what to do."

She strode across the bedchamber, rummaged amongst her things until she found her sewing scissors, and waved them triumphantly in the air. "Stand still, dearest. This won't take but a moment."

Harriett gasped. "Tilly! We can't *cut* it!"

"Certainly we can. There's nothing wrong with the gown that few judicious snips here and there won't fix."

"But it's one of Madame Dubois's original creations! It cost my aunt a fortune!"

ANNA BRADLEY

"Madame Dubois, my eye. I'd wager she's never been to France in her life. Have you noticed her Parisienne accent has a distinct tinge of the Yorkshire countryside about it? You can hear it whenever she's agitated."

"But she's London's most sought after modiste!"

"Then she should have known better than to put you in this gown to begin with. You're much too dainty for such an elaborate style. It overwhelms you, and makes you look as if you're a child playing dress up. Something simpler will suit you much better."

"Are you...are you cutting off the bows?" Harriett was watching in frozen horror as Tilly began carefully snipping away at the gown.

"Yes, but not to worry. I'm quite handy with my scissors, you know."

"But you'll cut a hole in it!" Harriet wailed. "How will I ever explain this to my aunt?"

"Nonsense. I'm not cutting the fabric, only the threads. I used to make over my sisters' gowns all the time, because we couldn't afford new ones every year." Of course, that was before Emmeline, Juliet and Helena had gone off and married earls. It had quite ruined her fun when they'd become such grand countesses.

Not that she begrudged her sisters their happiness, but she did miss them dreadfully. Oh, she visited them as often as she could, but Phee preferred to remain at home, and Tilly didn't like to leave her there alone.

Harriett was nothing like Emmeline, Juliet, or Helena, of course. Whatever naivete the Templeton sisters had once possessed had been tarnished by scandal, whereas Harriett remained as innocent as a daisy damp with morning dew.

56

"I don't think this is a good idea, Tilly." Harriett was twisting this way and that, trying to get a peek at what Tilly was doing. "What will I wear, if it ends up cut into ribbons?"

"I promise you it won't. Now hold still." Tilly snipped at the tiny stitches until the bodice was free of adornment, and showed off Harriett's trim figure to advantage. "There! That's much better. Turn around, and see for yourself."

Harriett had gone rather pale, but she did as she was told, and when she caught sight of her reflection, she slapped a hand over her mouth. "Oh my goodness, Tilly! I had no idea you were such an accomplished seamstress! Why, you could be a fashionable London modiste, if you wished."

"And put up with all those demanding belles and their shrieking mamas? No, indeed. Anyway, I didn't do anything magical. I merely removed some of the trimmings. The gown is beautifully cut, and doesn't need them."

Harriett twirled about in front of the mirror, her pale blue silk skirts whirling around her. "I can't believe how different it looks."

"Here, we'll do a sash like this, just in case I've missed any loose threads." She turned Harriett back toward the glass and tied a wide white ribbon around her waist.

"Why, it's like an entirely different gown! It's perfect, Tilly." Harriet turned and clasped her hands. "Thank you."

"Yes, it's a dramatic improvement, isn't it? Really, I don't know why the modistes insist on smothering everything in bows. As for your hair, we'll pull it back into a chignon, with just a few loose curls at your temples, like this, and secure it with your pearl bandeau. There we are!"

Harriett touched the cluster of curls, a shy smile on her face. "It's perfect."

"Good." Tilly squeezed Harriet's hands. "Now we may go downstairs."

The two of them made their way from the bedchamber down the stairs to the second floor ballroom, where several hundred of the *ton*'s most elegant aristocrats were waiting for them.

Along with one unconscionable rake, and a looming scandal.

Her first bit of business was to find the Earl of Prestwick, and once she did...

She'd do whatever she must—plead, threaten, lie, and yes, beg until he swore he'd keep their disastrous first meeting to himself.

~

"I HAVE no idea how you're meant to identify Lady Harriett *here*, Prestwick." Darby glanced around Lady Fosberry's ballroom with a puzzled frown. "All these chits look alike."

"How ungallant of you to say so, Darby." Not untrue, however.

He and Darby had been standing to one side of the ballroom for half an hour now, and in that time, dozens of young ladies had passed by. One of them *might* have been Lady Harriett, but damned if he could distinguish her from any of the others.

It had been six years, after all. She'd been little more than a child then.

He was certain to stumble upon her sooner or

later, but at the moment, he had a more pressing problem. He had to find the doxy who'd—

No, not a doxy! She *wasn't* a doxy, damn it.

The young lady, then, the guest of Lady Fosberry's who'd sneaked into his cottage and tossed a decanter's worth of absinthe in his face. He'd have no trouble recognizing *her* again, but there was no sign of her so far.

"Come, Prestwick. You must remember something about Lady Harriett. Is she fair, or dark? Tall, or short? Slender, or plump? What color is her hair?"

"Brown?" Yes, he was quite sure her hair was brown. "She's neither particularly tall, or short, neither slender or plump, but somewhere between the two."

"Well done. You've just described half the young ladies in the ballroom."

"What would you have me say, Darby? I never imagined I'd be required to distinguish her from hundreds of other young ladies. Why isn't she at Lady Fosberry's side? Surely, that would be a reasonable place to expect her to be?"

"Damned if I know. I've never been to a *ton* ball before, and now I see why. Rather a dull affair, isn't it, with all these pale-faced chits in their pastel gowns? How is a man meant to tell one of them from...ah, now wait a moment. What have we here?"

"What?" Kit followed Darby's gaze. "Who are we looking at?"

"Tall and slender, with chestnut-colored hair, wearing pink silk? She just came in." Darby nodded toward the entrance of the ballroom. "Delicious, indeed. She's restored my faith in pink gowns."

"Where? I don't see her."

"Just there, and she's... ah, ha! You're in luck, Prestwick! She's just joined Lady Fosberry. This is promising, indeed. Is she Lady Harriett?"

Darby kept whittering on, but Kit no longer heard him, because all his attention had narrowed to the young lady in the pink gown who'd just joined Lady Fosberry's party.

She was *not* Lady Harriett Fairmont.

She was the doxy who wasn't a doxy at all, but a graceful young lady in a pink silk gown, the tight bodice clinging to her curves, her thick chestnut waves pinned in an elegant chignon, a few stray wisps of hair brushing against the creamy skin at the back of her neck.

Good Lord. How had he ever imagined she was a doxy? She looked like another creature entirely, yet she was certainly his midnight intruder—

"You'd better ask her to dance at once, Prestwick."

There was no mistaking her, with those plump pink lips—

"Hurry, Prestwick, before her dance card is full. She'll have no trouble attracting partners."

And that smile, seductive and playful at once—

"For God's sake, Prestwick, what are you waiting for?" Darby turned to him with a frown. "Go fetch your countess, before someone else steals her away."

"That's not Lady Harriett."

"It's not? What damnable bad luck, Prestwick."

"Lady Harriett is next to her, talking to Lady Fosberry."

"The young lady in blue?" Darby peered at her for a moment, then shrugged. "Yes, I recognize her now. She lacks the panache of the lady in pink, but she's

60

quite pretty. I daresay she'll make you a proper countess."

"The lady in pink, Darby. Do you have any idea who she is?"

If anyone would know, it was Darby.

"I've never seen her before. I'd remember it if I had. Whoever she is, she's well acquainted with Lady Fosberry."

"Yes, it appears so." The four ladies stood together in an intimate knot, chatting with an ease that spoke of a long, close friendship.

Damnation. If he'd needed proof the Prestwick curse was real, here it was, right in front of him. He'd promised to marry one young lady, and compromised another, and of course it must turn out that the two of them were the best of friends.

What was he meant to do now? He couldn't marry both of them—

"The lady in yellow, Prestwick. She looks familiar, but I can't quite recall—" Darby broke off with a gasp. "Wait, is that...my God, it is! That's Euphemia Templeton!"

"Who the devil is Euphemia Templeton?"

"*Templeton*, Prestwick! Surely, you've heard of the scandalous Templeton sisters? Why, they're the scourge of every matron with a marriageable daughter in London. They're dear friends of Lady Fosberry's, and meant to be brilliant matchmakers, all five of them."

"Matchmakers? How ridiculous." Matchmaking was nothing more than a pastime for silly schoolgirls.

"Dear me, how the *ton* despises them!"

"Why should they?" There was nothing scandalous about them that Kit could see. "They look harmless enough."

Then again, looks could be deceiving. The lady in pink might not be a doxy, but she was certainly a vixen, and possibly even a madwoman. He still wasn't certain she hadn't tried to drown him in absinthe. Even thinking about the dousing she'd given him made his eyes burn.

"How can you not have heard of the Templetons, Prestwick? Although the worst of their scandal happened last year, while you were in Kent. Still, I'd have wagered that tale would make it all the way to Scotland."

"What did they do?" And why couldn't he tear his gaze away from the lady in pink?

"My dear Prestwick, what *didn't* they do? Emmeline Templeton, the next eldest after Euphemia, swept into London last season—a perfect nobody, mind you—and snatched up Lord Melrose right out from under everyone's noses. She's now the Countess of Melrose, much to the *ton*'s disgust."

"Well, what of it? It hardly seems fair to blame the lady for—"

"Oh, I'm not done, Prestwick. Not two months later, her sister Juliet attended a house party at the Earl of Cross's estate in Oxfordshire, and what do you think? She's now Lady Cross. Then the middle sister —Helen, I believe her name is, or Helena—has recently been elevated from the Earl of Chatham's governess to his *wife*. A *governess*, and she's Lady Chatham now!"

"What, all three of them became countesses in a single season?" That was a trifle unusual.

"Yes, indeed. It nearly sent London's matrons into

an apoplexy. The gossips claim all five of the Templeton sisters are sorceresses—fatal beauties who mesmerize gentlemen with their wicked wiles. It's utter nonsense, of course. How *delightful*, that they should be in London." Darby rubbed his hands together gleefully. "Perhaps the season won't be as dull as I feared."

Delightful? There was nothing delightful about it. "The lady in pink? Which Templeton is she?"

"Let's see. Emmeline, Juliet, Helena..." Darby counted the names off on his fingers. "Euphemia, the eldest, is the lady in yellow, so that leaves... Mathilda. The lady in pink must be Mathilda Templeton. She's the youngest."

"Mathilda Templeton," Kit repeated, staring hard at her.

"I'm going to ask her to dance before these other scoundrels fill up her dance card." Darby tugged on his coat, straightening it. "Perhaps she'll mesmerize me with her wicked wiles. I do hope so. My, I never dreamed the season could prove so entertaining."

"Wait, Darby." Kit caught him by the arm before Darby could rush off. "Ask Lady Harriett to dance the next two dances first, will you?"

"Lady Harriett!" Darby's lips turned down. "You dance with her, Prestwick. She's your countess."

Not yet, she wasn't, and she might never be, now. "I have some business with Miss Mathilda Templeton, and I'd just as soon Lady Harriett was kept out of the way until I've concluded it."

"Business, with Mathilda Templeton? Do tell, Prestwick."

"Later. Do this for me first, will you? There's a good fellow, Darby."

"Oh, alright, if I must." Darby let out a dramatic sigh, but he wandered off in Lady Fosberry's direction.

Meanwhile, Kit retreated to a quiet corner, his gaze fixed on Mathilda Templeton, her pink silk skirts tumbling gracefully around her, her heavy chestnut locks brushing her bare shoulders.

And waited for his chance to pounce.

SIX

"Here you are, girls! I'd begun to worry you'd miss the first dance of the evening." Lady Fosberry hurried forward to kiss Harriett's cheek. "Is this the gown we chose for your first ball? It's not as I remember it."

"Oh yes, Aunt, the very same." Harriett glanced at Tilly, biting back a grin. "If you recall, you insisted upon the blue one."

"So I did, and I was right to do so, because you look lovely, my dear. Mathilda, that shade of pink is stunning on you. I don't believe I've ever seen you look prettier."

"Thank you, my lady." Tilly fluffed the skirts of her gown. It had been a lucky choice, this gown, as she'd blend seamlessly with the dozens of ladies wearing a similar shade of pale pink.

A lady teetering on the edge of a scandal did well not to draw attention to herself.

"Come, girls, and I'll introduce you to Lord Griffiths and Lord Wrexham. They'll make excellent partners for the first dance."

"No thank you, my lady." Tilly linked her arm

with Phee's. "I believe I'll keep Phee company this evening."

Lady Fosberry stared at her. "You mean to say you won't dance, Mathilda? But it's your first ball of the season!"

Goodness, people did make a fuss about the season, didn't they? It was quite freeing, to have the luxury of not caring a whit about it. "I prefer observing to dancing."

Lady Fosberry huffed. "I hope you change your mind, Mathilda, but I know the futility of arguing with you. Come along, Harriett. I believe Lord Wrexham is smiling at you."

Phee turned to her once Lady Fosberry and Harriett were out of earshot. "Observing, Tilly? I've never known you to stand back and observe a single thing in your life. What are you up to?"

"Up to? Why, nothing at all." Just searching the ballroom for rakes. Or *rake*, rather. One specific rake, unless...perhaps he hadn't come tonight? She glanced around the ballroom, searching for an auburn head, and a pair of impossibly wide shoulders.

It wouldn't do to be caught unawares—

"Come, Tilly. You can't mean to stand about with me all night. Are you sure you won't dance?"

"Quite sure. I'm content as I am, I promise you. I'd much rather observe the company than attempt to muddle my way through a cotillion."

"You won't find a husband by observing, Tilly."

A lady could hope! "I daresay my chances of marriage won't be improved by dancing, as I look like a headless chicken when I do. Has Lord Wyle made his appearance yet?"

"Not yet, no. It's a pity we didn't get to meet him

at church on Sunday. I was hoping to gauge whether or not he's a proper match for Harriett."

"My dear Phee, every matron in London is angling after him. If he's a proper enough match for their daughters, then he's proper enough for Harriet. You're not having second thoughts about him, are you?"

"Oh, no, nothing like that. It's just matchmaking is all very well in theory, but as I tried to tell Lady Fosberry, I'm much better with numbers than I am with people. What if I've made a mistake, pushing the match?"

"You didn't push it, Phee. You merely suggested that based on your theories, Lord Wyle and Harriett might suit. It's up to them to decide if they do or not. If not, they'll discover it for themselves soon enough." Of course, they likely would suit, as Phee was an amazingly accurate judge of character.

"I suppose." Phee watched as Lord Wrexham led Harriett out to the floor. "But it's dreadfully nerve-wracking. I feel as if Harriett's future has been thrust into my hands."

"Harriett could find herself in far worse hands than yours. Between you and Lady Fosberry, she's destined for a happy ending."

"I hope you're right. We'll find out soon enough, I daresay, once Harriett and Lord Wyle dance together. One can learn a great deal from a single dance."

"Where *is* Lord Wyle?" Tilly glanced around the ballroom, searching for his golden hair, but she didn't see him. "Dash it, I was hoping he'd dance the first dance with Harriett. Whatever can be keeping him?"

"I daresay he'll turn up sooner or later."

"I suppose so. I do hope he arrives in time for the second—"

She broke off, the words dying on her lips.

He was here.

The infamous, the scandalous, the rakish Earl of Prestwick was *here*.

She rose to her tiptoes, her gaze locked on a shallow alcove on the other side of the ballroom, but dozens of heads were blocking her view. Heavens, must the ladies all wear such towering turbans?

Finally, the crowd shifted, opening a gap, but the alcove was now empty.

Lord Prestwick had disappeared.

If he'd ever been there at all. Perhaps he hadn't, and her guilty conscience was playing tricks on her, but how many gentlemen in London could boast such a distinctive shade of auburn hair?

"Who are you looking for?" Phee glanced across the ballroom with a frown.

"No one. Who would I be looking for? I don't know a soul in London aside from you, Harriett and Lady Fosberry." But a guilty heat was climbing into her cheeks. She despised lying, especially to Phee, but there was no question of Phee knowing of her, er... midnight encounter.

"But—"

"I beg your pardon, Phee, but I'm dreadfully parched. I believe I'll go fetch a glass of lemonade."

"You can't go charging across the ballroom by yourself, Tilly. This isn't Hambleden, where you may do as you please. We'll send a footman."

"No, no need. I fancy the walk." She darted off before Phee could stop her, wincing at her sister's shocked expression, but she simply couldn't rest until she'd made certain the man she'd just seen was nothing but a figment of her imagination.

She left Phee gaping after her, and began a slow circle around the ballroom.

If Lord Prestwick was here, she'd find him.

Except she'd rather not. She'd really quite prefer it if he wasn't here at all, but was off doing whatever it was rakes did. Wagering away his fortune at the gaming hells in Covent Garden, or dallying with his mistress.

Fanny. That had been her name, hadn't it?

Anywhere, but here in this ballroom.

Please, please don't let him be in this ballroom.

The plea echoed over and over in her head as she made her way from one end of the enormous room to the other, peeking around corners and into darkened recesses, as they seemed the sort of place a rake might hide.

There was no sign of him in her first sweep, and by the time she'd finished a second trip around the ballroom without seeing him, the tightness in her chest began to ease.

For once, scandal seemed to have made up its mind to leave her be, and thank goodness for it, because there was no telling the havoc a lady who'd managed to create a scandal in tiny Hambleden could do in a city like London.

One shuddered to think of it.

She caught her skirts in her hands and began to make her way back to Phee, who she'd abandoned in quite the rudest manner imaginable. But all would be well, now. If Lord Prestwick hadn't attended the first ball of the season, he wasn't likely to attend any others.

As for Phee, she'd make it up to her by being on her best behavior from this point forward, and—

"Good heavens!"

A large, gloved hand landed on her wrist, and with one quick jerk, tugged her into one of the alcoves that led onto a balcony. Cold air rushed through the thin silk of her gown, but it wasn't the chill that made her shiver.

It was the pair of dark eyes staring down at her. So dark, as dark as midnight, a thick lock of lustrous russet hair partially obscuring the left one.

"Miss Mathilda Templeton." He bent over her hand, his handsome lips curving in a wicked half-smile. "We meet again."

Oh, no. He *wasn't* a figment of her guilty imagination. No, he was *here*, and he'd taken the time to find out her name.

He stood before her in his elegant evening dress, his cravat such a blinding white its brilliance threatened to sear her retinas. A tiny sapphire stick pin sparkled among the folds, and his auburn hair was brushed into a gallant, if somewhat unruly Coup au Vent.

Had he always been so large? Goodness, he was so tall she had to take a step backward and tilt her head to get a proper look at him, but there they were, the dark eyes she remembered, gleaming down at her as if they could set her alight with a single glance.

She'd been alone in his cottage with him! *She*, alone with London's most notorious rake. Scandal had found her this time, hadn't it? It was bearing down on her, right on her heels, its fetid breath hot on her neck.

"Lord Prestwick. I didn't expect to see you this

evening." But of course, she had expected it. Deep down, underneath all her denials, she'd known he'd find her again, but she hadn't expected he'd yank her out onto a secluded balcony. "You have me at a disadvantage."

"I do, yes. It's rather a nice change from our first introduction. Unless, of course, you're hiding a bottle of absinthe behind your back."

The absinthe, again? "My, you do hold a grudge, don't you? If you recall, I was trying to help you." *Had* helped him, in fact, and now she heartily regretted it. "May I remind you, my lord, that I could have left you as you were?"

"It may have been better if you had." He gazed down at her, a grin twitching at the corners of his lips. "Why is it, Miss Templeton, that I suspect you make a habit of meddling in affairs that don't concern you?"

Ah, now there was a thorny question. The truth was, she *did* make rather a habit of meddling, often with disastrous consequences, but she wasn't going to say so to *him*. "An unconscious gentleman lying in a crumpled heap at the bottom of a flight of steps *does* concern me, my lord. Fortunately for you, as it turns out."

"I don't deny you did me a good turn. I'm grateful to you for it, but we both may yet come to regret it. We now share a secret between us, one that could prove damaging if the gossips get hold of it."

"Indeed. You did the right thing, coming here, my lord. Everyone knows the best way to keep a secret from the *ton* is to retire to a private balcony alone together in the midst of a ball, while three hundred people wander about on the other side of a flimsy silk curtain, hoping for a scandal."

He stared at her for a moment, eyebrows raised, then to her shock, he threw his head back in a laugh. "Perhaps I should have sneaked about your house while you were asleep, as you did to me. Would that have been less scandalous, do you suppose?"

Was he flirting with her? The Earl of Prestwick, flirting with *her*? "I didn't sneak, and you weren't asleep. You were *unconscious* from drinking an entire bottle of port."

"A bottle of port, and a decanter's worth of absinthe, yes. My valet was in fits over those green streaks. I'm afraid my shirt is quite ruined."

Were his lips twitching? Why, how dare he twitch at her? It was most inconvenient, that twitch, as it transformed his face, and now she was staring at his lips, imagining what a smile might do for him, and thinking about that kiss, the firm warmth of his lips moving over hers, and—

No, no, no! She wasn't going to think of that now. Or *ever*. Especially not at night.

"Your skull remains intact, my lord." She raised her chin. "I'd say you came off rather well."

"Mere details, Miss Templeton. But it makes no difference who's to blame for the debacle in which we now find ourselves—"

"You are, my lord. *You're* to blame."

He waved an arrogant hand in the air. "What matters, Miss Templeton, is what we do now."

My, he was grand, wasn't he? With that arrogant wave of his hand, and that maddeningly imperious tone. He was every inch an aristocrat, staring down that absurdly straight Grecian nose at her.

"Now then, Miss Templeton." He lounged back, resting his elbows along the balcony railing. "What do you propose we do about this inconvenient secret of ours?"

"*Do*? Why, I propose we do what one always does with an inconvenient secret. Keep it to ourselves. Really, my lord, you can't mean to say you came here tonight and dragged me onto a balcony to warn me to hold my tongue?"

"Would you have held it otherwise?" He gave her a lazy grin. "Forgive me, Miss Templeton, but silence doesn't seem to be a strength of yours."

Oh, he was dangerous, wasn't he, with those dark eyes and that teasing smile? She'd heard he could be devastatingly charming when he chose, and here was the proof of it, right here.

Not that *she* was charmed by him. Not in the least.

"You might have saved yourself the bother, my lord. I have a great deal more to lose than you do if that little tidbit reaches the ears of the *ton*." If Phee and Lady Fosberry found out she'd been alone in his cottage with him, they wouldn't rest until they'd badgered her into marrying the man.

"What an unexpected relief to find that we agree, Miss Templeton. I trust I won't find you wandering around my house uninvited at night again."

Oh, for pity's sake. "I didn't choose to be there in the first place! I only came to fetch Lucifer, and he wouldn't have been there at all if you hadn't left your front door open. So you see, my lord, this really is all your own fault."

"Ah yes, Lady Fosberry's dog. You're are aware, are you not, that his name isn't Lucifer? It's Lucius."

"Yes, but Lucifer is a far more appropriate name for him."

"I don't think Lady Fosberry would agree with you," he said, his grin widening.

Blast the man, he almost looked as if he were enjoying himself. "No, but Lady Fosberry doesn't have to know of it, does she?"

"Another secret, Miss Templeton? You seem to have a great many of them."

"What's one more, then? Now, if you'll excuse me, my lord, I'm certain my sister must be looking for me by now." She glanced down at his hand, which was still wrapped around her wrist.

"Of course." He released her at once.

She turned and peeked through the draperies, as it wouldn't do to emerge when someone was watching. Thankfully, there was no one nearby, but just as she was about to slip through, she paused and glanced back at him. "Pardon my curiosity, my lord, but I don't believe Lady Fosberry expected you in London."

He shrugged. "Plans change, Miss Templeton. I'm here for the season."

It was both an answer, and not an answer at once. Yes, he'd come for the season—he wouldn't have bothered with the ball tonight if he hadn't—but what could the season have to offer a rake like Lord Prestwick? Aristocratic gentlemen, for the most part, only participated in the season if they were in search of a wife, but he hadn't come for that. What irresistible attraction, then, could have lured him here, against every expectation?

Unless...no. There wasn't a single reason in the world she should assume he'd come for Harriett. Her imagination was simply running away with her, that was all.

Except he *had* just inherited the title. Earls were meant to take wives, and what better place to pluck a willing bride than from the family he'd known for years? Harriett was lovely, accomplished, and as sweet as a spoonful of treacle. Why wouldn't he want her as his countess?

Her heart took up frantic rhythm in her chest, and her palms went damp inside her white silk gloves.

"You look distressed, Miss Templeton." He straightened from the railing and took a step toward her. "Is something amiss?"

This was the point at which she should leave well enough alone, but she'd been plagued by that strange moment she and Lady Fosberry had shared in the carriage, after they'd spotted Lord Prestwick outside St. George's.

I wonder, she'd said. *I wonder...*

What had Lady Fosberry wondered? God help her, but she simply couldn't resist a bit of prying. Just a tiny prick or two, that was all. "Are you well acquainted with Lady Fosberry, my lord?"

"We're not acquaintances at all, Miss Templeton, but friends of long standing. Our families have known each other for decades."

Decades? That long? "Have, ah..." She swallowed. "Have you, indeed?"

"I don't know why you look so surprised. Prestwick House is just next door, after all. Lord Fairmont and I spent every summer together here in Hampstead Heath when we were growing up. Are you acquainted with Lord Fairmont, Miss Templeton?"

"No. That is, I know of him, of course, but he's

been away from England for some years now, and I've never been introduced to him."

"Ah." He stepped closer. "But I believe you *are* acquainted with Lady Harriett, are you not, Miss Templeton?"

When had he gotten so close? Dear God, he was looming over her, impossibly tall and broad and arrogant. The charming grin was gone. He gazed down at her with hooded dark eyes, every trace of teasing vanished.

But he wouldn't intimidate *her*, for all that his shoulders were as wide as a mountain range. She raised her chin. "Very well acquainted, yes. I consider her to be one of my dearest friends."

"She's a lovely young lady. I quite look forward to sharing a dance with her this evening."

A dance? Oh, no, that wouldn't do at all. It was a quick leap from one dance to two, and from there to a carriage ride, then it would be a stroll along The Serpentine, and the next thing she knew, Harriett would be betrothed to London's wickedest rake.

Why, a single dance tonight could doom Harriett to a marriage with Lord Prestwick! "I'm afraid that's impossible, my lord. I, ah, I just left Harriett, and her dance card is already full."

"Lady Harriett is fortunate to have such a vigilant friend in you, Miss Templeton, but I daresay she can spare a dance for *me*."

"At the expense of some other gentleman? I don't see why she should."

He gazed down at her, his dark eyes glittering, that odd smile still toying with his lips. "Because, Miss Templeton, Lady Harriett is my betrothed."

"*Betrothed!*" Surely, she'd misheard him? "She can't be!"

"She can, I assure you. She *is*."

"But how... Harriett never mentioned a word of this betrothal to *me*." And that was to say nothing of the fact that Harriett hoped to soon be betrothed to Lord Wyle!

"No? Well, ladies do have their secrets, do they not? Perhaps you're not as well acquainted with Lady Harriet as you imagine."

"I... you..." Dear God, what was happening? "You can't expect me to believe you're betrothed to Lady Harriett when neither Lady Fosberry nor Harriett has breathed so much as a word about it."

He shrugged. "You may believe what you like, Miss Templeton. It's of no consequence to me, but the facts are what they are. Lord Fairmont and I reached an agreement some years ago regarding his sister becoming the next Countess of Prestwick. Lady Harriett and I were promised to each other, and I've come to London to collect my bride."

It was a lie. It had to be, only...

Lady Fosberry had been agitated when she'd seen Lord Prestwick outside St. George's—more so than a chance meeting warranted. As for Lord Prestwick, he was a scoundrel, to be sure, but would he go so far as to lie about a betrothal? Why would he go to the trouble, when such a lie was so easily disproven?

She cast one last look into his eyes— eyes as dark as midnight. If he was lying, she couldn't see it there.

Had Harriett lied to her, then? Or...no! No, that wasn't it.

Harriett didn't know a thing about the betrothal!

Lord Prestwick had mentioned Harriett's brother only—
he'd spoken of the agreement between himself and Lord
Fairmont—but he'd never said a word about Harriett.

But Lady Fosberry knew. She *must*.

Why had she asked Phee to matchmake Harriett,
then? Why was she so assiduously encouraging a
match with Lord Wyle?

Dash it, none of this made any sense!

She must speak to Lady Fosberry at once. A ballroom stuffed to the rafters with gossiping *ton* was
hardly the place to discuss Harriett's secret betrothal,
if such a thing existed, but it simply couldn't wait.
"Forgive me, my lord, but I'm certain my sister must
be looking for me by now."

She backed away from him, stumbling over her
own feet.

He smiled, but it was more a baring of teeth than
anything— a wolf on the verge of devouring a sheep.
"Of course, Miss Templeton."

He took a step toward her, and she came up
against the draperies behind her, the silk brushing
against her back.

"Allow me." He reached over her, his gloved fingertips a mere breath away from touching her bare
shoulder, and tugged the draperies aside.

She didn't hesitate, but whirled around and
darted through them, back into the safety of the
ballroom.

CHAPTER
SEVEN

K it shoved the silk draperies aside and strode through them, his gaze on Mathilda Templeton, who was flying across the ballroom in a streak of pink silk, her destination unmistakable.

She was scurrying like an outraged squirrel directly toward Lady Fosberry.

Soon enough, her ladyship would have an earful about the Earl of Prestwick's nefarious designs upon her innocent niece. Perhaps he shouldn't have mentioned the betrothal to Miss Templeton, but it had been worth it to see the meddlesome chit's eyes go as round as robins' eggs.

"Good God, Prestwick, what did you say to Mathilda Templeton?" Darby caught up to him halfway across the ballroom, and fell into step beside him. "She's fleeing as if the devil himself is on her heels."

Not the devil, no. Just a wicked earl. "Perhaps Miss Templeton should be more careful who she trifles with."

"Perhaps it's *you* who should be more careful,

79

Prestwick, because whatever you said to her, she's repeating it to Lady Fosberry right now."

She was, indeed. Even at this distance, he could see her whispering in Lady Fosberry's ear. "I merely confided my intentions regarding Lady Harriett to her."

Darby stopped, his eyebrows shooting up. "Was that wise?"

"Lady Fosberry is well aware of my agreement with Lord Fairmont." Whether she intended to hold him to it or not...well, that was what he needed to find out. Either Lady Harriett or Mathilda Templeton was destined to become the next Countess of Prestwick. The question was, which of the two of them would satisfy the demands of the curse? "Did you dance with Lady Harriett?"

"Yes, and I'll tell you, Prestwick, it was the longest bloody quadrille of my life. She's a frightened little mouse of a thing. I was certain she'd burst into tears at every moment."

"Meek, is she?"

"As a lamb, yes."

Damn. No gentleman, not even a wicked one, wanted to court a terrified young lady who was likely to blanch at the very sight of him.

But perhaps he wouldn't have to.

Fairmont had evidently left the matter of his sister's engagement to Lady Fosberry, and if she didn't approve the match...

His gaze wandered back to Mathilda Templeton.

Whatever else one might say of her, she wasn't terrified of anything, or anyone.

"Now, Miss Mathilda Templeton, on the other hand," Darby said, as if he'd read Kit's mind. "There's not a bit of the lamb in her, is there? That glare she's sending you right now, Prestwick! It's a wonder you haven't disintegrated into a pile of ash."

That *was* a glare, by God. "She looks as if she'd like to bury a blade in my chest, doesn't she?"

Darby didn't answer. He was glancing about, a puzzled frown on his face. "Er, Prestwick, have you noticed—"

"What reason could Mathilda Templeton possibly have for glaring at me like that?" That is, he *had* mistaken her for a doxy, but she'd nearly *drowned* him. Surely, they were even?

"I beg your pardon, Prestwick, but—"

"She's a menace, Darby." A menace with exceptionally lovely blue eyes, but a menace nonetheless. "I've never encountered a more troublesome—"

"For God's sake, Prestwick! Look around you, man. Everyone is staring at us!"

"Staring? Don't be absurd, Darby. Why would they be..." He trailed off, blinking. A crush of bodies surrounded them, but a pathway had cleared before them, and dozens of curious gazes were following their progress across the ballroom. "What the devil?"

"Lady Ingoldsby looks as if she'd like to devour you," Darby muttered under his breath as they passed the lady in question.

She did, which was odd, indeed, as she'd given him the cut direct when they'd met at the theater last winter. Whatever offense he'd committed then was evidently forgiven now, as the lady's lips stretched into an eager smile when he caught her eye, and she quickly nudged her daughter forward.

"I warned you this would happen, Prestwick," Darby hissed through clenched teeth.

"*What*? What's happening?" Why was every matron in the ballroom grinning at him?

"Just keep moving." Darby nudged him forward.

"Christopher!" Lady Fosberry reached out her hand to Kit as they approached. "Oh, dear, I mean Lord Prestwick, of course. I beg your pardon, my lord, but it's dreadfully difficult to remember to call you by your title when I've known you these twenty-five years or more."

"You may call me whatever you wish, my lady. Such old friends need not stand on ceremony." Kit bowed over Lady Fosberry's hand, risking a quick glance at Mathilda Templeton as he did.

She was watching him with narrowed eyes, her mouth pressed into a tight line. He cleared his throat, and wrenched his gaze away from her. "I don't believe you're acquainted with Mr. Darby, my lady."

"I am not." Lady Fosberry took Darby in from head to toe. "Mr. Darby's reputation precedes him, however." It would have been an insult from anyone else, but the twitch of Lady Fosberry's lips took the sting out of her words. "This is Miss Euphemia Templeton." She gestured to the lady in yellow who stood beside her. "Lord Prestwick, and Mr. Darby."

Euphemia Templeton, who appeared to be a great deal quieter and more reserved than her younger sister, offered them a polite smile. "Lord Prestwick, and Mr. Darby."

"Miss Templeton." Darby dipped into a smooth bow, and held out his hand. "Will you favor me with a dance?"

"Oh, I..." Euphemia Templeton stammered, her cheeks going red. "I didn't intend to—"

"Nonsense, Euphemia." Lady Fosberry nudged her forward. "Of course, you must dance."

There was little Miss Templeton could do then but accept Darby's hand, and permit him to lead her out to the floor.

"It's a pity Harriett didn't know you'd be here this evening, my lord, otherwise she would have saved you a dance," Lady Fosberry went on.

"I beg your pardon, my lady?"

"Harriett, Lord Prestwick." Lady Fosberry nodded toward the dance floor. The musicians had just played the last notes of a lively Scotch reel. Lady Harriett had been dancing with Lord Wyle, but instead of returning her to her aunt, Wyle swept her into the Sussex Waltz.

Two dances? Was Wyle angling for Lady Harriett? Because she could hardly do any better than Wyle. He was this season's Nonesuch, and every young lady in London wanted him.

His gaze drifted back to Mathilda Templeton, who wasn't taking any pains to hide her dislike of him, with that fierce scowl on her pretty lips. A reluctant twinge of admiration pricked him. She *was* a menace, just as he'd told Darby, but despite her dainty appearance, the girl had a spine of steel.

"... afraid her dance card is already full this evening," Lady Fosberry was saying. "It's a pity, as I'm certain she would have been delighted to dance with such a dear old friend."

"Hmm? Oh, yes. That is a pity."

"But no matter, my lord. Miss Mathilda here is *longing* for a waltz. Aren't you, Mathilda?"

"Who, *me*?" Mathilda glanced at Kit, aghast. "A waltz, with *Lord Prestwick*?"

"Of course, with Lord Prestwick." A small smile rose to Lady Fosberry's lips. "He's standing right here, is he not?"

"I've no desire to waltz with Lord Prestwick. Indeed, I can't think of anything that would please me less. Why, I'd rather have a tooth pulled than—"

"That's quite enough, Mathilda." Lady Fosberry rapped Miss Templeton on the arm with her fan. "I do beg your pardon, my lord. Mathilda is a trifle, er...reserved, I'm afraid."

Reserved? Mathilda Templeton was as reserved as a feral cat, but it wasn't as if he could refuse to dance with her. "Of course, my lady." He offered Mathilda Templeton his hand. "Would you care to—"

"Lady Fosberry!" A small, round lady in acres of apple green silk with an enormous peacock feather in her turban was bustling toward them, tugging a young lady by the arm. "I'd quite despaired of finding you, but here you are, at last!"

Lady Fosberry, who hadn't stirred from her corner of the ballroom all evening, blinked in surprise. "Lady Henry. How do you do?"

"Very well indeed, my lady. My dearest Nancy here was just saying that your entertainments are always the most delightful of the season." Lady Henry cast a sidelong glance at Kit, and pushed her daughter forward. "Weren't you, Nancy?"

"I... I..." Nancy stammered, a flush in her cheeks. "That is, I—"

"And Lord Prestwick! How do you do, my lord?" Lady Henry rushed on, before her daughter could get another word out. "It's wonderful to see you! It's been ages, has it not?"

"Er, yes. I daresay it has." Not long enough, however. He could have happily endured another age without the affliction of Lady Henry's company. Hadn't she called him a disgraceful rake the last time they'd met?

But here she was, one shove away from toppling her daughter into his lap.

It was beginning to look as if Darby was right, after all. London's matrons appeared eager to forgive his sins, now he was the Earl of Prestwick.

"I can't tell you how delighted I was when I saw you arrive this evening, my lord. I said to Nancy, my goodness, isn't that Lord Prestwick? How handsome he looks!" Lady Henry let out a girlish giggle. "Didn't I say so, Nancy?"

"Yes, mama." Nancy peeked at Kit, her blush deepening.

A brief silence fell, then Lady Henry let out a gusty sigh. "The Sussex Waltz! How delightful! This is Nancy's favorite song, you know, my lord."

Well, that was plain enough. There was little he could do after such a broad hint as that but offer his hand to the daughter. "Perhaps Miss Henry would like—"

"My dear Lady Henry, I thought that must be you!"

They all turned at once to find Lady Arundel descending upon them out of nowhere, her five daughters trailing at her heels. "How do you do, Lady Fosberry? Such a splendid ball! You quite outdo yourself."

"Thank you, my lady. That's kind of you to—"

"Lord Prestwick!" Lady Arundel interrupted, turning to Kit. "I don't believe you're acquainted with my daughters. Miss Arundel, Judith, Alice,

Betty, and Priscilla." She jerked the eldest forward, thrusting her before Kit as if she were a sweetmeat on a tray.

"Er, how do you do, Miss Arundel, Miss Betty—" Wait, which one was Betty, and which one Alice? They were all pale-faced chits, each of them dressed in varying shades of pale blue. Damned if he could tell them apart.

"Lord Prestwick!" Another shriek rent the air then, and a third lady appeared, waving her fan wildly in the air. "Oh, Lord Prestwick!"

He watched in horror as she bore down on them, towing two young ladies in her wake. God above, what was happening? Where had all these chits come from, and was he meant to dance with all of them?

"Oh, dear. It's Lady Calvert, of all people. She's the worst of the lot."

The whisper came from his left, and he glanced down to find Mathilda Templeton's face turned up to his, her dark blue eyes filled with unholy glee. "Lady Calvert," he repeated faintly. "Do I even know Lady Calvert?"

"You will, very soon. You have my deepest sympathies." The grin she gave him was so wicked, it rivaled one of his own. "Do enjoy the rest of your evening, Lord Prestwick."

She slipped into the crowd then, the press of bodies swallowing her, and an instant later, she was gone.

~

TILLY WAITED until the last of Lady Fosberry's guests had gone home, and Harriett and Phee had gone off

to their beds before she made her way to her ladyship's private sitting room.

As she'd expected, Lady Fosberry was waiting for
her there. She went in, taking care to close the door
behind her.

It wouldn't do for anyone to overhear them.

"Goodness, balls are exhausting, are they not?"
Lady Fosberry dropped onto a settee with a sigh.
"Fetch us some sherry, won't you, Mathilda?"

Tilly went to the sideboard, poured a measure
into each of two glasses, then handed one glass to
Lady Fosberry before seating herself in a chair. "Harriett doesn't know about the betrothal to Lord Prestwick, does she?"

Lady Fosberry stared down into her glass for a
moment before shaking her head. "No. I saw no
reason to tell her. I expected she'd be betrothed to
another gentleman by the end of the season, and it
never need come up. Of course, that was before
Christopher appeared for the season."

It was true, then. There *was* an agreement, just as
Lord Prestwick had said. "You're not in favor of the
betrothal, then?"

"No. If I'd had any notion James meant to make
such a foolish arrangement, I would have dissuaded
him. I didn't approve of the match when I learned of
it, and I don't approve of it now."

"Thank goodness." Tilly sagged against the settee. "What can Lord Fairmont have been thinking,
betrothing his sweet sister to a scoundrel like Lord
Prestwick?"

"He was neither scoundrel nor Lord Prestwick at
the time the agreement was made."

"Well, he's both now."

"Indeed, he is not." Lady Fosberry took a judicious sip of her sherry before meeting Tilly's eyes. "Christopher has made some questionable choices, Mathilda, but he's no scoundrel. Not at his heart."

Not a scoundrel? Why, the man was the very definition of a scoundrel! Lady Fosberry's long friendship with the family had blinded her to Lord Prestwick's true nature.

"Ah, I see you doubt me, Mathilda, but I'd wager every penny I have on the goodness of Christopher's heart. Oh, I don't say he's hasn't earned his rakish reputation, but there's a difference, my dear, between a man who's callous and cruel by nature, and one who is simply...misguided."

That was rather a generous interpretation of Lord Prestwick's character. "If that's so, then why should you object to his marrying Harriett?"

"Why, because they don't suit, of course. Lord Fairmont loves his sister very much, and would never betroth her to any man he believed would make her unhappy, but the agreement was made years ago, and James is no matchmaker. I can't in good conscience let the match go forward."

"But won't Lord Fairmont be angry when he returns to England and discovers his sister isn't the Countess of Prestwick?" He was meant to return soon. No one knew precisely when, but perhaps before the season was over.

"Not if she's the Countess of Wyle, which I think likely. Lord Wyle appears to be quite taken with Harriett."

He did, yes. It wouldn't do to count one's chickens, of course, but anyone could see Lord Wyle admired Harriett. "Any fond brother must prefer Lord Wyle over Lord Prestwick."

"You quite mistake Christopher's character, my dear. I would have thought one who's own family has been so viciously slandered by spiteful gossip might show more compassion." Lady Fosberry's tone was mild, but she held Tilly's gaze. "Of all people, Mathilda, you should know things are rarely as the gossips claim."

Oh, dear. She *did* know that, better than anyone, and her cheeks heated at the rebuke. "You're right. That was unkind of me. I beg your pardon."

"It's quite alright." Lady Fosberry reached over and squeezed her hand. "It's just that I feel rather protective of Christopher. He's the last of the Prestwicks, you know, now his uncle is dead. He's alone, and rather lonely, I think."

"He's not alone," Tilly said absently. "He has Fanny."

A long silence followed, but it wasn't until she looked up and saw the astonishment on Lady Fosberry's face that Tilly realized her blunder. "I... that is, I mean—"

"Tell me, Mathilda. How do you happen to know the name of Lord Prestwick's former mistress?"

"I, ah—Harriett must have mentioned it to me." As soon as the words tumbled from her lips she wanted to bite her tongue out. Harriett—sweet, naïve Harriett—was meant to have told her about Lord Prestwick's scandalous mistress?

Oh, what a dreadful blunder! Lady Fosberry would surely demand to know the truth, and the entire garden escapade would spill from her lips, and

Lady Fosberry would tell Phee, and Phee...oh, Phee would be so disappointed in her!

"I see." Lady Fosberry set her glass aside and folded her hands in her lap. "I don't believe you told me, Mathilda, how you and Lord Prestwick became acquainted tonight."

"The usual way one does at a ball." Tilly waved a careless hand, as if that explained everything, but the only way a gentleman might become acquainted with a lady at ball was if a common acquaintance introduced them. Lady Fosberry was their only common acquaintance, and presumably she was aware that she hadn't made the introductions.

Lady Fosberry pinned her sharp gaze on Tilly, but she said only, "Christopher needs a wife, and it won't be Harriett."

"I daresay he'll find one soon enough. A dozen marriage-minded mamas descended upon him tonight. I've never seen a man more horrified in my life, though I don't know why he should be surprised at it. Scandalous reputation aside, he's just what every lady in London is clamoring for." Indeed, if he weren't such a scoundrel, he'd very likely be the season's Nonesuch, instead of Lord Wyle.

"Oh? How so?"

"Well, he's...he's very... that is, he's...." Tilly took a gulp of her sherry. "He's an earl, for pity's sake, and not...entirely unattractive."

"Ah, so you *do* think him handsome, Mathilda?"

"I don't think of him at all!" But the denial was too quick, and too vehement, and Lady Fosberry's lips curved in a sly grin. "Oh, for pity's sake. Very well, then. I don't see that there can be much debate on the subject. Lord Prestwick is, objectively, very handsome."

Very wicked, as well, no matter how much Lady Fosberry insisted otherwise.

"Poor Christopher is in for trying season, I'm afraid." Lady Fosberry shook her head. "His trouble will be too many applicants for his hand, not too few."

"I daresay he'll manage."

"I don't see how. What does a rake know about choosing a proper match from the hordes of young ladies who will throw themselves at him this season? I daresay he'll become frustrated before the first week is out, and insist upon having Harriett."

Insist upon having Harriett! Oh, she didn't like the sound of that at all. "What do you mean?"

"I mean, Mathilda, that every mama in London is determined to make her daughter the next Countess of Prestwick, and Christopher doesn't have the first idea what to do with any of them."

"But Harriett doesn't have to have him! She can refuse his hand." Oh, dear. She'd gone a bit shrill.

"She can, yes, but she may well find herself labeled a jilt if she does. As much as we may wish otherwise, Christopher is right when he says Harriett is promised to him."

"But the promise was made years ago, before he became an unconscionable rake!" For pity's sake, why didn't anyone else seem to realize what a dreadful scoundrel Lord Prestwick was?

"That will make no difference to the *ton*, I assure you. I suppose we'll just have to hope for the best." Lady Fosberry rose to her feet and made her way to the door. "Goodnight, Mathilda."

ANNA BRADLEY

Once she'd gone, Tilly dropped back down onto the settee, her head whirling.

What if Lady Fosberry was right? What if Lord Prestwick grew impatient with the chaos fluttering around him, and decided the quickest way to put an end to his misery was to wed Harriett?

She thought of Harriett's dreamy smile as she'd looked into the glass tonight, the pretty flush in her cheeks as Lord Wyle twirled her around the ballroom this evening. She was well on her way to a happy-ever-after, but it would all come crashing down in an instant if she were labeled a jilt.

Dear God, they were only a week into the season, and already they were teetering on the edge of disaster. Whatever else happened, Harriett could not be left at the mercy of Lord Prestwick.

Something must be done, and quickly.

But what?

CHAPTER
EIGHT

K it mounted the front steps of Fosberry House and gave the door a smart rap just as a single faint chime from a grandfather clock struck the one o'clock hour.

He'd timed his arrival perfectly. Calling hours had just begun.

The door opened, and Watkins, Lady Fosberry's butler appeared on the other side, flawless in his dark blue livery, and offered Kit a bow. "Good morning, Lord Prestwick."

"Watkins."

"This way, my lord. The ladies are in the drawing room."

Kit followed Watkins down the corridor, cursing under his breath as his heart began to flop wildly in his chest with every step he took toward the drawing room.

Really, the heart was the most ridiculous organ imaginable. One of the advantages of being a rake was never having to bother with the blasted thing.

If he'd been madly in love with the lady he was promised to, he might have endured it calmly

93

enough, but all this absurd flopping about wasn't because of Lady Harriett.

Oh, he'd done just as an eager swain was meant to do the morning after a ball. He'd sent Lady Harriett an impressive bouquet of white damask roses and lilies from the Prestwick hothouses, and he was dutifully presenting himself at her doorstep, but it wasn't Lady Harriett who occupied his thoughts this morning.

No, it was Mathilda Templeton, damn her. Mathilda Templeton, who'd doused him with absinthe, spoiling an exceptionally fine linen shirt in the process. Mathilda Templeton, who could hardly contain her glee when Lady Henry and Lady Arundel had thrust their daughters upon him at the ball last night.

He'd been obliged to dance with all of them, God help him.

The only young lady he hadn't danced with was Mathilda Templeton.

Well, and Lady Harriett, of course. Perhaps if she'd been bedeviling him since he'd arrived in London as Mathilda Templeton had, he wouldn't keep forgetting her.

He didn't even *like* Miss Mathilda, but as it happened, a man didn't need to like a lady for her to creep under his skin, and damned if she wasn't burrowing deeper with every moment that passed.

It was most uncomfortable.

But he wouldn't permit her to distract him this time. He wouldn't leave the drawing room until he knew whether or not Lady Fosberry approved of his courtship of Lady Harriett.

Surely, he could do that much? He'd been charming enough, once upon a time.

"Lord Prestwick," Watkins announced, then withdrew.

"Christopher." Lady Fosberry beamed at him as he entered the drawing room. "It's kind of you to call on us this morning."

"My lady." He offered her a bow, then turned to the elder Miss Templeton. "How do you do this morning, Miss Templeton?"

"Very well, my lord, thank you." She gave him a polite nod, then went back to the lace she was mending.

He turned, his traitorous heart thumping, and there, seated on a silk settee the same color blue as her eyes was Mathilda Templeton, a demure smile on her lips, and every one of her rich chestnut curls in place. "Good morning, Miss Mathilda."

"Lord Prestwick." She inclined her head, but didn't raise her gaze from the embroidery in her lap.

She'd exchanged last night's pink silk ballgown for a plain white cambric dress with some sort of frill around the neck. There was no reason it should have held his attention— young ladies all over London were wearing similar plain white day dresses as they received their callers, but for some reason he couldn't seem to tear his gaze away from that ridiculous frill, and the way the soft white cambric brought out the creaminess of her skin—

"My niece will be disappointed she was obliged to miss your call this morning." Lady Fosberry poured out a cup of tea, and offered it to him. "Tea, my lord?"

"Yes, thank you." He cast a surreptitious glance around the drawing room as he took the saucer. How had he not noticed that one face was missing from this sweet, domestic circle? Lady Harriett was nowhere to be seen. "I do hope Lady Harriett isn't unwell," he murmured.

"Not at all. She's perfectly well, only a trifle fatigued." Lady Fosberry gave him a bright smile. "The first ball of the season can be a bit overwhelming for young ladies who've never been to London before, as you can imagine, Christopher. We thought it best if she rested this morning."

They thought it better she *rested*? During calling hours, after the first ball of the season?

He glanced from Lady Fosberry to Mathilda, but she'd become intensely preoccupied with picking an invisible speck of dust from her skirts, and didn't meet his eyes.

Ah. He'd been hoping for a sign from Lady Fosberry regarding his interest in Lady Harriett, and here it was. She didn't like the match.

"I daresay it was too much dancing," Mathilda said, breaking the awkward silence that had fallen. "Do you know, Lord Prestwick, that Harriett danced every dance last night?"

"Indeed, I did know. If you recall, Miss Mathilda, you informed me of it last night." She'd chased him off before he'd gotten within twenty paces of Lady Harriett.

"Oh, yes. I remember now. The only guest who danced more than Harriett was *you*, Lord Prestwick." She kept her gaze on her lap, but her lower lip was caught between her teeth, and the corners of her mouth were twitching.

Was she laughing at him?

"It was excessively kind of you to dance with all five of the Arundel sisters, my lord."

She *was* laughing at him, by God, and enjoying herself immensely, the infuriating chit.

"Harriett was ever so grateful for the lovely flowers you sent this morning," she went on. "Indeed, they were so pretty, and their scent so heavenly I couldn't resist taking them up to her bedchamber, so she might enjoy them." She glanced up from rearranging her skirts, her blue eyes dancing. "Lord Wyle's weren't nearly so nice."

"We don't compare one gentleman's flowers with another's, Tilly," Lady Fosberry said, though she appeared more amused than anything else.

"Not to the gentleman with the lesser flowers, no. I wouldn't dream of saying such a thing to Lord Wyle, I assure you."

Lady Fosberry snorted, but Miss Templeton frowned at her sister. "That's quite enough, Tilly."

Of course, that gentle scold wasn't enough to quiet Mathilda. "Lady Fosberry tells me you have the most delightful hothouses at Prestwick House, my lord."

"Are you interested in flowers, Miss Mathilda?" He didn't know a blessed thing about flowers, but he and Mathilda Templeton had some unfinished business between them. What better place to discuss it than Prestwick House? "I don't pretend to know much about the hothouses, or the flowers and plants there, but I'd be pleased to show them to you, Miss Mathilda."

There, that sounded harmless enough.

She hadn't expected the invitation, nor did she look pleased by it. She was biting her lip as if she wished she'd never mentioned the blasted flowers at all. "It's, er, kind of you to offer, Lord Prestwick, but I daresay my sister won't approve of—"

"Nonsense," Lady Fosberry interrupted. "Let her go, Euphemia. Lord Prestwick will take good care of her, won't you, my lord?"

He glanced down at Mathilda, and curled his lips in a slow smile. "Indeed."

"I don't see any harm in it." Miss Templeton smiled at her sister. "Just for a short time."

"Of course." Kit offered Mathilda his arm. "Shall we?"

"It appears we shall." She rose to her feet, and reluctantly accepted his arm.

He only hoped his hothouses—and Prestwick House itself—was still standing by the time Mathilda Templeton was finished with it.

∼

"I'VE NEVER SEEN finer flowers than yours, my lord." She sniffed delicately at a white bloom. "It's scent is reminiscent of coconut. It looks like a gardenia, but the placard says it's a Rose of May narcissus."

"I suppose it must be, then." How much time had passed since he'd last spent time in the hothouses? Years. Even when he'd lived here with his uncle, he hadn't appreciated them, and now, he wondered why. Mathilda Templeton was a troublesome baggage, but she was right about the flowers. They *were* pretty.

"I've never heard of that variety, but then that's the wonderful thing about having a hothouse, is it not? So many exotic flowers!" She strolled down the narrow pathway, pausing now and then to study a bloom that struck her fancy. "Prestwick House must be very grand."

"Yes."

She didn't look at him, but ran her fingertips over the ruffled edges of the narcissus's white petals. "Why do you stay in the cottage?"

She was the first person to ask him that question. Darby had alluded to it—he'd said something about Kit hiding there—but even he hadn't *asked*.

It was strange, that she should be the first.

He hadn't set foot in Prestwick House since Freddy had died there. Even now, a year later, he couldn't say for certain that he'd ever darken the doorstep again. "Because it isn't mine."

She might have said any number of things then. That of course the house was his. That he was the earl, and earls didn't stay in shabby cottages when they had grand estates at their disposal.

But she didn't. Instead, she said, "I wasn't lying about your bouquet. Harriett really did prefer your flowers to Lord Wyle's."

"But you *were* lying about everything else?"

"I wouldn't say *lying*, precisely."

"Oh? What would you say, Miss Mathilda?"

She lifted one shoulder in a shrug. "That I haven't lied to you, my lord, but I haven't told you the entire truth, either."

"Perhaps you should do so now, then." She wouldn't, of course. She'd hint, and stall, and prevaricate until he couldn't be sure of a damned thing.

"Very well, if you insist on it." She drew in a deep breath, and turned to him, her gaze meeting his. "The truth, Lord Prestwick, is that you're not going to marry Lady Harriett."

Well, not so much prevarication, after all. "Oh? And why is that, Miss Templeton?"

"Because you and Harriett don't suit."

If she hadn't looked so earnest, he might have laughed, but there was no humor in those dark blue eyes, and no dissembling. "It's not your place to make that judgement, Miss Mathilda."

"You're quite right, my lord. It's Harriett's decision, and she's made it."

"Ah, but that's where you're wrong. It's not her decision at all. As I told you last night, Lord Fairmont made the decision for her years ago. What if I still wish for the match?" He didn't, but Mathilda Templeton didn't need to know that.

For now, it suited him that she didn't.

"Then I'm sorry for you. Harriett doesn't wish for the match, and she, not Lord Fairmont will be compelled to spend the remainder of her days with you if the match goes forward. Thus, her opinion matters a great deal more than his does."

"What I don't understand, Miss Mathilda, is why you should think *your* opinion matters at all. This has nothing to do with you. Or does it?"

She gazed up at him, her blue eyes wide. "I beg your pardon?"

"Does Lady Harriett's disinclination to entertain my suit have anything to do with that unfortunate incident between us at the cottage the other night?"

Another lady would have dropped her gaze, and perhaps backed away from him, but Tilly Templeton wasn't, it seemed, the sort of lady who flinched at a challenge. "No, my lord. That has nothing at all to do with it."

There was nothing in her expression that would

indicate she was lying— no telltale blush on that smooth white cheek —but perhaps she was simply an accomplished liar. "How can you be certain?"

"Because I never said a word about it to her."

From what he knew of young ladies, that seemed exceedingly unlikely. "What's this really about, Miss Templeton? Why are you going to such lengths to prevent this match? Is it that you don't wish for your dearest friend to marry a drunken scoundrel?"

A faint smile crossed her lips. "Are you a drunken scoundrel, Lord Prestwick?"

He had been, once, and not so very long ago, either. As for what he was now, well...God only knew. "Ask anyone. They'll all tell you I'm the wickedest rake London has ever seen."

She regarded him for a moment, then shook her head. "I daresay you're not as wicked as they all claim you are."

He stared at her. No one had ever given him the benefit of the doubt before, least of all a young lady who'd seen him sotted, bloodied, unconscious and reeking of sour port. "That's, ah, surprisingly generous of you to say."

"It's not generosity, my lord, but simple rationality. Gossips are prone to exaggeration. I know that well enough from my own experience."

Her experience? He would have said she was a young lady of no experience at all.

"As for why I'm going to such lengths to prevent a match between you and Harriett, the answer is quite simple, my lord. I wish to see my friend happy."

"She has as much chance of being happy with me as with any other gentleman."

"No, Lord Prestwick, she doesn't. She doesn't love you."

"*Love?*" Good Lord. Like so many young ladies fresh from the country, she was painfully naïve, her head no doubt filled with romantic girlish nonsense about the season, and love, and marriage. "The season isn't a romantic escapade, any more than marriage is a fairy tale."

Not for Lady Harriett, not for Mathilda Templeton, and not for him, either.

"No, but neither should it be a torment. As I said before, my lord, you and Harriett don't suit. She won't make you any happier than you will her, and there's really no need for you to marry *her*, when we saw at the ball last night that you might have your choice of dozens of other young ladies in London."

"Ah, but that's the very problem, you see. How am I to decide between them? I haven't the first notion how to choose a proper wife. If you won't help me, I'll end up married to one of the Misses Arundels."

She choked back a laugh. "I doubt that, my lord. All five of them were quite terrified of you, as was Lady Henry's daughter, the poor thing. But there are dozens of young ladies in London this season who might do for you."

"Is that so? Which young ladies would those be?"

She shrugged. "As to that, I can't say."

"No?" He drew closer, the sweet scent of the flowers tickling his nose. "I daresay you could, if you put your mind to it. In fact, I think you're just the lady to help me choose a bride. Mr. Darby tells me you and your sisters are all brilliant matchmakers."

She went still for an instant, staring at him, then shook her head. "You can't be serious, my lord."

"Oh, but I am serious, Miss Mathilda." She'd taken a step backwards, but he pursued her, holding those dark blue eyes with his. "Perfectly so. What better way to reconcile me to the loss of Lady Harriett than to help me find a replacement?"

"But you can't...." She swallowed. "Do you mean to say you want me to matchmake *you*?"

"That's precisely what I mean." He took another step toward her—not too close—but close enough to see into her eyes. "As a matchmaker, you're uniquely qualified to assist me, Miss Mathilda."

It was the truth. She *was* uniquely qualified to assist him. Not because she was a matchmaker, but because she alone, of all the young ladies in London, was the only one who could help him lay the curse to rest.

He didn't need a matchmaker. He'd already chosen his countess.

Except with the way things stood between them now, she'd never have him. She'd already proven how wily she was, and he didn't fancy a season's worth of skirmishes with her.

But a courtship, disguised as a matchmaking scheme? It was devious, unscrupulous, and utterly brilliant.

While she was matchmaking *him*, he'd be courting *her*.

She opened her mouth, then closed it again. People spoke of being speechless—struck dumb with shock—but he'd always thought it a figure of speech.

Until now.

At last, she found her tongue. "You don't need me, my lord. If you find the field of, er...hopeful young ladies too overwhelming, you can always put off marriage until next season. I can't think why you're in such a rush to wed, in any case. You can't be more than thirty years old."

Thirty! Presumptuous chit. "I'm twenty-eight, but I don't wed only for my own sake, Miss Mathilda. I have a child to think of."

Her eyes went wide. "A child? You have a...oh, dear."

Well, he could hardly blame her for thinking what she was so clearly thinking, could he? "He's not my child, but my Uncle Freddy's son. Samuel Henry Egan, two months old, and already an orphan. Would you doom the poor mite to another year of a motherless existence?"

"A motherless..." She trailed off. "I, ah, I don't...I think, Lord Prestwick, that I'd better return to Lady Fosberry now."

He didn't argue, or make any move to stop her, but only inclined his head. "As you wish, Miss Mathilda, but do think about what I said, won't you? I think you're, er...just the lady I need."

She didn't reply, but turned without a word and hurried through the door, her white skirts flying behind her as she rushed across the grounds. He watched her go, then stood at the window for a long time afterwards, an uneasy prickling in his chest.

His courtship of Lady Harriett was at an end, but the curse was still very much alive, and Freddy's son Samuel as much in danger of falling victim to it as he'd ever been. He couldn't bear to leave an innocent child to suffer the punishment for a century's worth of Prestwick sins.

Samuel was Freddy's son. Freddy's *son*, and the only family member Kit had left.

He'd never abandon him.

He still needed a wife, and it wouldn't be Lady Harriett. He couldn't regret it. Miss Mathilda was right—they didn't suit, and the prospect of marriage with her brought him no pleasure.

As for Mathilda Templeton...

She drove him mad with her sharp tongue, and those blue eyes filled with mischief. She was a vixen, a termagant, and the very last sort of lady he'd ever imagined himself marrying, but he was far from indifferent to her.

Even if he had been, it wouldn't have mattered.

He'd compromised her. Not intentionally, no. It had been an accident, but that would make no difference to the *ton*, if the story ever came to light.

Then, of course, there was the curse.

A compromised young lady was a compromised young lady, regardless of the circumstances, and the only cure for ruination was marriage.

And if his conscience was now pricking at him for luring her into a courtship through trickery, it wasn't because of the shadows he'd seen in her eyes just before she'd fled.

It wasn't that, at all.

CHAPTER
NINE

"A picnic, of all wretched things." Darby took in the scene before them, his lips turned down in a scowl. "You do realize, Prestwick, that we could be enjoying a perfectly civilized meal at White's right now?"

"Only you could find fault with a picnic, Darby."

"We're obliged to sit on the *ground*." Darby cast a dark glance at the lawn spread out before them. "These are new pantaloons! Rusticating is the most barbaric thing imaginable, Prestwick."

Kit sighed, but to be fair, if their roles had been reversed, and it was Darby who was dragging him through every dull entertainment of the season in order to avoid an ancient curse that may or may not be real, he would likely have complained, as well. There was little about the London season to amuse a rake.

"Come now, Darby, it's not as awful as you make it out to be. Just look." Kit swept his hand over the pastoral scene before them. "Can't you find anything here to please you?"

It was rare warm spring day, and Lady Fanshawe

had made the most of it by moving her breakfast party outdoors to the wide expanse of lawn that rolled out in a ribbon of verdant green, transforming what would no doubt have been a dull, stuffy affair into a delightful picnic.

At least, her guests appeared to be finding it delightful.

Young ladies lounged on the blankets spread out across the lawn, their pastel skirts fluttering in the light breeze. Dozens of harried servants dashed about, delivering wicker picnic hampers to each party. It was a pretty scene, and if he could judge by the laughter drifting on the breeze, everyone was enjoying themselves.

Everyone but Darby, who was frowning at the picnickers as if he were witnessing a beheading. "Not a blessed thing. I should be comfortably asleep in my bed right now, like a proper scoundrel, although...is that Miss Edgerley, just there by the fountain? She's amusing enough."

Darby didn't wait for an answer, but wandered off toward Miss Edgerley, who looked tremendously pleased to see him—quite as pleased as her mother was displeased, by the sour look of her—but Lady Edgerley might fend for herself, as he had his own business to attend to.

If anyone had told him a week ago that he'd soon be chasing Tilly Templeton, he would have called them mad. But here he was, searching the lawn for Lady Fosberry's party.

Unfortunately, attempting to pick Tilly out from the sea of young ladies in straw hats and pastel gowns was like trying to separate grains of sand in a desert. Aside from one young lady, who was gesticulating so wildly one could hardly fail to notice her, one was very much like every other—

Wait. Those riotous chestnut curls...

He reached up to shade his eyes from the sun, but he needn't have bothered.

Of course, it was her. Who else but Tilly Templeton could be surrounded by dozens of other young ladies, and still distinguish herself? He watched her for a moment, puzzled. How did she always manage to draw his eye? It wasn't as if she was doing anything untoward, yet the sway of her slender body as she spoke, the graceful movements of her hands made it impossible for him to see anyone else.

He couldn't fault her for lack of passion, could he? It was like witnessing a bolt of lightning illuminating the sky.

Lady Fosberry and Euphemia Templeton were lounging on the blanket at her side, laughing at her antics. Lady Harriett was at her feet, her white skirts spread demurely over her legs, not a hint of ankle showing, the very picture of pastoral innocence.

And beside Lady Harriett sat Lord Wyle.

He'd certainly wasted no time marking his territory, had he? They weren't yet two weeks into the season, and already the man had made it clear he intended to court her.

Perhaps he imagined no other gentleman would bother, once he made his intentions known, and he was likely correct. All the *ton* adored Wyle, and why shouldn't they? He was everything a proper English gentleman should be.

At least, as far as anybody knew.

Darby claimed he'd heard a rumor last winter that Wyle was in financial difficulties after a run of back luck at Hazard. But Darby was a shameless gossip, and most of the stories he repeated were too fantastical to be believed. That the gentleman *The Times* had crowned this season's Nonesuch was a secret gamer seemed fantastical, indeed.

Whatever the case, Lady Harriett seemed delighted to receive his attentions. Well, he wished them joy. She was a sweet young lady, and he'd been fond of her when she was a girl, but he must still have a bit of the rake in him, because he didn't care for shy young ladies with soft voices and sweet blushes.

He preferred ladies with a bit more...ferocity.

His gaze drifted back to Tilly Templeton. She would be his countess, yes, but as he'd told her yesterday, love didn't have anything to do with marriage. It was fortunate he didn't have a heart to lose, because the unlucky gentleman who fell in love with her would be driven mad within a fortnight.

He crossed the lawn, pausing only to bid Lady Fanshawe a good morning before making his way over to Lady Fosberry's party, where Tilly was telling some story. He only caught the tail end of it, but it had the whole party laughing.

"...but as I told Phee at the time, she couldn't properly scold me for it, as it was only a very small fire, you know, and no harm was done." She wore a mischievous little smile on her lips that halted him for an instant in his tracks.

What sort of innocent young lady had such an alluring smile as that? Pure temptation, the sly curve of those pink lips.

She must have sensed his gaze, because she turned. The smile froze on her face, then vanished entirely, a stiff, polite mask taking its place. "Lord Prestwick. How do you do?"

"Miss Mathilda. Lovely day for a picnic, is it not?"

"Prestwick." Wyle gave him a curt nod, his lips tight.

Kit offered him a careless nod in return. "How do you do, Wyle?"

"Do sit down, won't you, Lord Prestwick?" Lady Fosberry patted the empty space on the blanket beside her. "It's fortunate you've arrived, as you're just in time to settle an argument for us."

"Oh?" He settled himself in the offered place, taking care not to assault anyone with his long legs. "What argument is that?"

"Euphemia and Harriett maintain that the pleasantest thing about a picnic is lounging on a blanket and eating syllabub, but Mathilda and I are of the opinion that—"

"Haven't we settled this argument already?" Lord Wyle gave Lady Harriett a smooth smile. "I believe we agreed that Miss Templeton and Lady Harriett have the right of it."

Good Lord, that fawning smile of Wyle's was enough to turn his stomach.

"We agreed upon no such thing, because *you*, Lord Wyle, abstained from offering your opinion." Lady Fosberry gave a disapproving sniff.

"Then I'll state it now, shall I? I agree with Lady Harriett."

"Do you indeed, Wyle?" Kit murmured. "How shocking."

"Alas, my lord, it's too late to state your opinion now. You had your chance, and you squandered it. I will hear from Lord Prestwick instead." Lady Fosberry turned to him. "Is the pleasantest thing about a picnic the lounging and syllabub, my lord, or do you maintain, as Mathilda and I do, that a vigorous walk in the fresh air and warm sunshine is the entire point of the thing?"

He despised lounging—already his arse was numb from trying to sit still on this blasted blanket, and syllabub was a vile pudding. It tasted like cream-flavored air.

But if he'd still been courting Lady Harriett, he never would have said so. He would have proclaimed an undying passion for lounging and syllabub, because what was courtship, after all, but a series of pretty lies?

But he *wasn't* courting Lady Harriett any longer. He was courting Mathilda Templeton, and with her, there was no need to lie, or put himself into the same category as a toady like Wyle, with that ingratiating smirk on his lips.

For the first time since his call on Lady Fosberry yesterday, the tightness in his chest eased, and he was able to draw a deep, cleansing breath of fresh air into his lungs.

"Well, Lord Prestwick?" Lady Fosberry tapped the back of his hand with a gloved finger. "Your answer?"

He gave her his most charming grin. "I can't imagine this could have caused such an argument between you all, when the answer is patently obvious."

"Is it, indeed? Do tell us your opinion, my lord." Tilly had edged closer—so close a fold of her skirts had fallen over his pantaloons, and God help him, he *liked* it. He wanted her eyes, and all her attention, on him.

"Why, just look, Miss Mathilda." He waved his hand around, taking in the glorious blue sky above them, so rare in London during the early spring, and the lush carpet of green beneath them. "Who could prefer a spoonful of syllabub to a ramble in such perfect weather as this?"

A brief silence fell, but just as he began to fear he'd agreed rather too vehemently, Tilly let out a surprised laugh. "Well said, my lord."

And just like that, whatever misgivings he had drifted away like petals on the breeze.

"Indeed, Lord Prestwick, most sensible of you." Lady Fosberry gave him an approving smile, her eyes dancing. "Though I must confess I quite adore syllabub, myself."

"I do, as well." Tilly rose to her feet and dusted the stray bits of grass from her skirts. "Don't eat it all, if you please, as I intend to indulge myself when we return."

"Return?" Euphemia Templeton had been rummaging in the hamper, but now she looked up. "Where are you going, Tilly?"

"Lord Prestwick and I are going for a wander, of course." She reached down, offering her hand to him. "Shall we, my lord?"

It was an odd gesture— ladies did not offer their hands to gentlemen —yet it had been done with such a natural friendliness, he couldn't resist accepting. He reached up and clasped her fingers, his much larger palm swallowing them in one gulp, and allowed her to tug him to his feet.

He offered her his arm. "Where do you wish to wander?"

"Lady Fanshaw mentioned there's a rose garden

just past those trees there. It's too early for roses, of course, but it looks like a pleasant walk, doesn't it?"

"Perfectly pleasant, yes."

Neither of them spoke as they made their way across the lawn toward the arbors visible just past a thick row of shrubbery, but there was nothing strained in it. Had he ever enjoyed a companionable silence with a lady before? If he had, he couldn't recall it.

"Will you attend Lord Colville's ball on Wednesday?" she asked at last.

"Yes, I suppose I must." The threat of the endless round of balls, picnics and musical evenings in his future hung over him like a cloud, dimming his pleasure in the sunny day.

"You don't sound pleased about it, my lord."

"I don't care much for balls."

"No, neither do I. They're dreadfully tedious."

"I thought all young ladies were mad for balls." But then, she wasn't like any other young lady he'd ever known, so why wouldn't she be different in this, as well?

She shrugged. "I daresay most young ladies are, but balls during the London season weren't really meant for ladies like me."

Ladies like *her*? What did that mean? "I don't understand. I would think you'd be as welcome at a ball as any other young lady."

She was quiet for a moment, then, "You mentioned matchmaking yesterday. You needn't pretend you don't know the rest of the rumors about my family, my lord. Everyone in London has heard of the scandalous Templetons."

There was no point in acting as if he didn't know

what she meant. "Very well, then. I've heard of your family."

"You know then, that the *ton* believes us to be witches or sorceresses who have worked our wicked wiles on the unsuspecting gentlemen of London." She cast him a sidelong glance. "The entire *ton* has their eye on you this season. With such high stakes, there's a very real risk to my reputation if I agree to help find you a countess, and I wouldn't bring another scandal down on my family's head for the world."

For an instant he hesitated, but there would be no scandal this time. Tilly Templeton would end the season as the Countess of Prestwick, and no one would dare breathe a word against her then.

He'd make certain of that.

If they went ahead with this wild scheme, there would be no turning back, but what was there to turn back to? A silent cottage, a silent estate in Kent, an orphaned infant, and an ancient curse?

No, there was only moving forward now, so he drew in a breath, and leapt. "I swear to you that no harm will come to you, your name, or your family's reputation. You have my word on it."

She wasn't looking at him, but kept her gaze focused on the shrubs straight ahead. "If I agree to help you, do I have your word that you won't pursue Harriett?"

That was an easy promise to make. "You do. As you said yesterday, Lady Harriett and I don't suit. She seems to favor Lord Wyle, and I've no desire to make Lady Harriett unhappy by pressing an unwanted suit upon her."

"That's good of you, my lord. I do think she's grown rather fond of Lord Wyle."

"Then I wish her every happiness. The trouble, Miss Templeton, is that I still must marry this season, but—"

"But every young lady in London is desperate to become the next Countess of Prestwick, and you have no idea how to choose one of them over another."

Her grin took the sting out of the words, and he felt his own lips curling helplessly in response. For all Tilly Templeton's wild antics, she did have a fetching smile. "Something like that, yes."

She didn't answer right away. They resumed their walk, and for some moments the only sound was the crunch of his boots heels over the gravel pathway, then she said, "In answer to your question from yesterday, I *don't* wish to doom an orphan child to another year of a motherless existence. If you still wish for my help, Lord Prestwick, I'll give it to you."

They'd reached the row of shrubs, and she paused, plucked one of the glossy leaves, and crushed it in her hand. She leaned down to sniff it, then held out her hand to him. "It smells like ginger."

There was something vaguely improper about the gesture, but he caught her wrist, raised her hand to his nose, and inhaled. "More like nutmeg, I think. What is it?"

"Allspice, perhaps? It looks a bit like the allspice in Lady Fosberry's garden, but I'm not terribly knowledgeable about plants. They all look the same to me. My sister Emmeline could tell us. She's a botanist, and knows all there is to know about growing things."

Emmeline. She meant the Countess of Melrose, of course, who'd caused a most spectacular scandal when she's snatched Lord Melrose out from under the nose of every other ambitious young lady in London.

The gossips might say what they liked about the Templeton sisters, but one couldn't argue with their results. "It's kind of you to agree to help me with my, ah...countess problem, Miss Mathilda."

"Tilly, my lord." She smiled. "I prefer Tilly."

He'd never thought of Tilly Templeton as sweet before. Wily, yes. Tart-tongued, certainly. Meddlesome, to be sure. But there was something so sweet about that smile, so pleasing, that the last of his misgivings melted into the mild spring air. "Very well, Tilly. Then you must call me Kit."

"Kit." She tried the name out, rolling it on her tongue. "Well then, Kit. I'll get to work at once, and will have a list of names for you before Lord Colville's ball later this week."

He nodded, then reached out to pluck another of the leaves from the shrub. He rolled it between his fingers, then brought it up his nose. "Clove. It's neither ginger nor nutmeg, but clove."

He held out his hand to her, and she leaned close, her face near enough he might have stroked her cheek with his fingertip, and inhaled. "So it is."

CHAPTER
TEN

Tilly snatched up the paper spread out atop her lap desk and crumpled it in her fist, despair creeping over her.

She'd hardly stirred a muscle since Lady Fosberry and Harriett had left with Lord Wyle to take a drive down Rotten Row. She'd been sitting on this settee for so long she'd likely sprung roots by now, and all she had to show for it was one name.

A single, paltry name.

Lord Colville's ball was mere hours away. She'd promised Lord Prestwick— Kit —that she'd have the list ready for him this evening, but after days of agonizing over it, here she was, no further along than she'd been when she started.

Somehow, not a single young lady in all of London seemed to be the right match for him.

What was she going to do? For pity's sake, she should have known better than to get herself into such a quandary after that fiasco with Miss Groves, but she... well, perhaps she'd wanted to believe she wasn't so very different from her sisters, after all.

It had begun well enough. At first, she'd been certain that any one of the dozen young ladies on her list would suit Lord Prestwick, but upon further consideration, doubts began to creep in.

This young lady was too arrogant for him, and that young lady too serious. This one was as dull as a Sunday sermon, and that one could talk of nothing but shopping and fashions.

Lady Emily Durham? Too silly. Miss Colchester? Too meek. Lady Charlotte Greville? Too high in the instep, and a vicious gossip, besides. Any one of the Arundel sisters would leap at the chance to have him, but even a scandalous rake deserved better than to be cursed with Lady Arundel as a mother-in-law.

On and on it went, until one by one, she'd crossed nearly all the names off the list again.

As it turned out, matchmaking a formerly scandalous earl wasn't as easy as she'd imagined it would be. At least, not *this* formerly scandalous earl. He wasn't, well...aside from their disastrous first meeting, he was nothing like she'd always imagined a rake would be.

Lady Fosberry had told her that Kit had a good heart. She hadn't believed it, but he'd released Harriett from their betrothal readily enough, and he'd been utterly sincere when he'd told her he had no wish to make Harriett unhappy.

There was kindness in him, and a vulnerability she never would have thought to find in a handsome, aristocratic gentleman. And she hadn't missed the shadow of pain in his dark eyes when he'd told her Prestwick House wasn't truly his.

He was lonely, just as Lady Fosberry had said, and he deserved a worthy wife. Love matches were as rare as diamonds, but surely there must be one young lady in London this season who would make him a proper countess?

One young lady who would deserve him?

She glanced down at her list with a sigh. The only name left was Lady Cressida Crawley, but she was far from an ideal match for Lord Prestwick. Her bright blue eyes might be the toast of London, but the head to which they were attached was as empty as a sieve.

She threw her pencil down with a huff. "Phee, if you had to matchmake a rake, how would you go about it?"

"A *rake*?" Phee glanced up from the book on her lap. "Why in the world would I ever have to matchmake a rake? I don't even know any rakes."

"Yes, you do. Mr. Darby, the gentleman you danced with at Lady Fosberry's ball is a rake."

"Mr. Darby, a rake?" Phee frowned. "Surely not. I've never observed him to behave as anything less than a perfect gentleman. I believe you're mistaken, Tilly."

For pity's sake. How could Phee have spent the past two weeks among the *ton*, and not have overheard even a scintilla of gossip? "I assure you, I'm not. Lady Fosberry told me herself that Mr. Darby does not always act as a proper gentleman should."

"My goodness. I had no idea." Phee set her book aside with a sigh. "As for matchmaking a rake, it's immaterial. Rakes don't wish to marry, so I'd never have an occasion to matchmake one." She took up her book again, as if the matter were settled.

Well, that wasn't much help, was it? "Yes, but for argument's sake, Phee. It's all very well for you to matchmake Harriett and Lord Wyle. Two more perfect people never existed. A truly talented matchmaker should be able to find a proper match for the worst scoundrel in London."

"What's gotten into you, Tilly? Are you attempting to matchmake a rake?"

"*Me*, matchmake a rake? Dear me, no!" Tilly laughed a bit too loudly. "Why, I don't know the first thing about matchmaking! The one time I attempted it, it was an utter disaster. Have you forgotten about the...the Incident?"

"That business with Miss Groves, you mean? That was *not* your fault, Tilly." Phee dismissed Miss Groves with a flick of her fingers. "You couldn't have known she was promised to another gentleman when she persuaded you to help her ensnare Mr. Hugo. The lady lied to you."

Miss Groves had lied, but Tilly had been foolish enough to be taken in by her, and poor Mr. Hugo had ended up with a broken heart. It was her first attempt at matchmaking, and it had been an embarrassingly public disaster.

If nothing else, the Incident had proven that she, unlike her four sisters, hadn't any talent as a matchmaker. They were all brilliant like her father had been, quick-witted and talented, whereas she...*wasn't*.

She wasn't clever like Phee and Emmeline, or intuitive like Helena, and neither was she charming and amusing like Juliet. Her only talent was causing scandals. God above, what had she been thinking, imagining she could matchmake Lord Prestwick? She'd make a mess of his affairs, and everyone in London would find out about it—

"If you're not matchmaking, then what is that you're working on?" Phee nodded at the crumpled papers on the lap desk.

"This? It's nothing!" Tilly slapped her hand over the page. "It's, ah, it's just a letter to Helena, that's all."

"Helena is asking how one goes about match-making a rake?"

"No. In her last letter she asked who we'd danced with at Lady Fosberry's ball, so naturally I mentioned you'd danced with Mr. Darby, and that got me thinking about rakes, and... that's all."

"That's all, is it?" Phee glanced at Tilly's hand, still spread protectively over the paper, and raised an eyebrow. "You've simply developed a sudden, inexplicable interest in rakes, then?"

"It's not the rakes I'm interested in, Phee. It's the matchmaking, but only in the, er, academic sense."

"Very well, then. I suppose I'd matchmake a rake just as I would any other gentleman. A tarnished reputation isn't likely to affect a man's prospects, after all, particularly if he's an aristocrat with a tidy fortune. Not like a lady, who will be ruined forever by the merest breath of scandal, regardless of whether she did anything wrong."

This last was said with enough bitterness that Tilly jerked her gaze from the page she'd been scribbling on to her sister's face. It wasn't like Phee to speak with such harshness. "Phee? Are you alright?"

Phee patted her hand, but her smile was strained. "Yes, I'm well enough, just a trifle homesick. I'm...not fond of London."

No, she wouldn't be, would she? Their mother's scandal had happened during Phee's first—and last—season. Mama had jaunted off to the Continent with her married lover, leaving Phee and their father behind to face the shame and humiliation that followed. To make matters worse, the gentleman who'd been courting Phee at the time had abandoned her without a second glance.

All that London had ever offered Phee was scandal, and heartbreak.

Now here she was, tempting another scandal with this risky business with Lord Prestwick.

She must get this list done! It was the one thing she'd promised Lord—Kit, dash it—she'd do. It had been a mistake to promise even that, but she wouldn't go back on her word now.

She'd give him the list at the ball tonight, and tell him she couldn't do anything more for him. She didn't like to do it, but she couldn't trifle with Phee's peace of mind in this reckless way. If Phee were to be hurt again, she'd never forgive herself, and it wasn't as if she were a *real* matchmaker, in any case.

"London is a wicked old place, isn't it?" She squeezed Phee's hand. "But we'll be back in Hambleden before you know it."

~

"ARE we going to hide out here on the balcony for the entire ball, Prestwick, or do you intend to venture into the ballroom at some point?"

He wasn't *hiding*, for God's sake. "I don't know what you're on about, Darby. I simply came out onto the balcony to take in a breath of fresh air, that's all."

Yes, he'd remained here for the last half-hour since then, peering through the draperies like a child hiding from a thrashing, his gaze fixed on the ballroom, but he wasn't hiding.

Only, er...observing.

"No need to explain yourself to me, Prestwick. I'd hide too, if every chit in London was determined to catch me in the parson's mousetrap." Darby shuddered. "Young ladies can be rather terrifying, can they not?"

Kit didn't give a damn about the young ladies. He cared only for one young lady, but she hadn't yet appeared. He twitched the edge of the curtain open again, pressed his eye to the gap, and made as thorough a study of the ballroom as he could manage with one eye.

There were dozens of young ladies with brown hair scattered about, but none with Tilly's particular shade of rich, warm brown, like chestnuts and brown sugar roasted over an open—

Chestnuts and brown sugar? What the devil?

Tilly's hair was *brown*, and her eyes *blue*. That was all.

He pulled the draperies closed with a grunt of disgust and strode to the railing, sucking in a breath of the sharp, cold air. Where was she? It was nearly half-ten—

"Good evening, Lord Prestwick."

The voice was soft, but he whirled around as if at a pistol shot. There, dressed in a jonquil ballgown that brought out the dark gold threads in her hair, stood Tilly Templeton, and he... well, all at once, he couldn't quite catch his breath. "I—good evening."

She ducked through the draperies, and pulled them closed behind her. "I've been searching everywhere for you. What are you doing, hiding back here?"

Darby snorted, and Kit shot him a quelling look. "I beg your pardon. I was *not* hiding. I was..." Well, damned if he knew what he'd been doing, though it must be said that searching ballrooms for Tilly Templeton had become quite a habit of his.

"It's alright, my lord. There's nothing wrong with hiding. How do you do, Mr. Darby?" she added, turning to Darby with a smile.

"Much better, now you've arrived, Miss Mathilda." Darby offered her an elegant bow. "I couldn't imagine what had Prestwick so out of sorts, but I see now that he's been waiting for *you*."

Kit could feel Darby's questioning gaze on him, but this wasn't the time to satisfy his friend's curiosity. "Hadn't you better adjourn to the ballroom, Darby? I saw more than one young lady in need of a partner."

"Yes, alright. I'm going." Darby slipped past the curtain, muttering something about wallflowers under his breath.

Kit hardly heard him. Now that Tilly was here, she had all of his attention. "I'd begun to fear you wouldn't come tonight, after all."

"We were rather late leaving the house. I'm afraid we spent too much time lingering at the looking glass."

"Worth every moment," he murmured, taking her in from head to toe. "Jonquil suits you."

The look he cast her must have been more frankly admiring than he'd realized, because the most charming blush he'd ever seen rushed into her cheeks. "Thank you, my lord."

"Kit, Tilly. Not my lord. We agreed, remember?"

"Yes, of course. I, ah, I brought the list I promised you, Kit."

"Ah, yes." The list of his potential matches. But

not one of the young ladies on her list would ever become his countess, because his countess was standing before him now in her fetching jonquil silk gown, wisps of dark hair brushing the bare skin of her neck. "May I see it?"

"Yes." She grasped the fingertips of her left glove and began to draw it off.

Slowly. One finger at a time, the clinging white silk giving way inch by tantalizing inch, revealing the creamy, warm skin beneath. He cleared his throat. "What, ah...what are you doing?"

"I didn't want anyone to ask me about it, so I hid the paper inside my glove."

Dear God. He'd watched dozens of ladies strip their gowns from their backs while he lounged on a bed, but he'd never seen anything as erotic as Tilly Templeton sliding her gloves from her fingers.

They were gloves, for God's sake. *Gloves.* But it didn't matter. By the time she was done, his mouth had gone dry, and his hands were shaking.

"Here it is." She held up her hand. A folded piece of paper was pressed into the center of her dainty pink palm. "It's not a long list—only three names."

"Am I so hard to matchmake, Tilly?" He took a step toward her, his voice low and teasing.

"No! No, of course not. I just thought we'd wait and see which of these ladies you preferred before we went any further."

"Very well." He tore his gaze away from the delicate wash of pink on her cheeks as it drifted down her throat, and held his hand out for the paper. "Lady Cressida Crawly," he read aloud.

"Yes. I own she's not precisely..." She bit her lip. "That is, she's a trifle, er, whimsical."

Whimsical? Certainly she was, if by whimsical one meant as silly as a giggling schoolgirl, and as empty-headed as a peahen. "Would we call her whimsical?"

She winced, dropping her eyes. "Perhaps not *precisely* that, but she does have lovely blue eyes."

He touched his fingers to her chin and lifted her face to his. "I've seen much lovelier blue eyes than hers."

For the first time since they'd met, Mathilda Templeton appeared to be struck speechless. Her throat worked, but she said nothing, only gazed up at him with wide blue eyes so vastly superior to Lady Cressida's, it was like comparing a humble bluebird's wing to an endless stretch of summer sky.

They gazed at each other, neither of them speaking, another fetching wash of color scalding her cheeks until at last he took pity on her, and glanced back down at the list. "Miss Fitzjohn?"

"Yes. She's not as glamorous as Lady Cressida, but she's clever, and kind." Tilly swallowed. "She'd make you a sweet, affectionate wife."

"And does that matter to you, Tilly? That my countess be sweet to me?"

She caught her breath as his fingers drifted lightly down her neck. "No proper matchmaker would doom a gentleman to a cold marriage, my lord."

"That's good of you, Tilly." He pressed a gentle finger into the hollow of her throat, a bolt of heat surging in his belly when her pulse leapt against his fingertip. "I'd much prefer an ardent, warm-hearted wife, if one can be had."

"I...of course." She cleared her throat. "Lady Anne Wilmott."

Lady *who*? "I beg your pardon?"

"Lady Anne Wilmott, my lord." She nodded at the paper in his hand. "The last name on the list."

"Oh. Yes, of course. Lady Anne is..." But he couldn't think of a single word to describe Lady Anne —not while he was touching Tilly, her skin impossibly soft and warm under his fingers.

He was bound to wed her, yes—the circumstances demanded it—but somehow, from the moment he'd pried open eyes burning with absinthe to the moment she'd appeared on the balcony tonight, glowing like the sunrise in her bright silk, she was the only lady he could think about, the only lady he could see.

"Lady Anne is your best match, my lord. You should dance with her first, then Miss Fitzjohn, and if neither of them suits, Lady Cressida."

"And if none of the three of them suits, Tilly? What then?" There wasn't a thing wrong with Lady Anne, or Miss Fitzjohn, or even Lady Cressida, by most gentlemen's reckoning.

But none of them was Mathilda Templeton.

To his surprise, the color drained from her cheeks, and she drew away from him.

"Tilly? What's the matter?"

"I can't...I can't go on with this matchmaking scheme after tonight. I never should have agreed to it in the first place. With the way scandal seems to chase the Templetons, the risk of shame to my family is simply too great."

"Ah. Your family has had some bad luck, haven't they?" He let her go, his hand falling away from her face. "The Prestwick family knows all about bad luck."

Her brows drew together, but she said only, "Shall we? Lady Anne awaits, my lord."

He shook his head. "No."

"No? You won't dance with Lady Anne?"

"I won't dance with any of them, until I've first danced with you, Tilly."

"*Me*? Why should you wish to dance with me?"

She looked so amazed, a startled laugh fell from his lips. Did she really not see it? Could she not look into his eyes, and see her own reflection there? It seemed impossible she didn't know how alluring she was, but he said nothing, only held out his hand to her. "Because you're my friend, are you not?"

She blinked up at him, her eyes so wide he thought he might fall into them, but then a shy smile crossed her lips. "I've never had a gentleman friend before."

He caught her hand in his, and raised it to his lips. "Then I suppose I'll be your first."

CHAPTER
ELEVEN

"Lord Wyle truly is the most engaging gentleman I've ever met. Did you not find him engaging this evening, Tilly?"

"Oh, yes, terribly engaging, indeed. Quite a study in gallantry." Tilly was lying on her back on her bed, her eyes wide open, and had been for some time despite the late hour, and not only because Harriett had been gushing about Lord Wyle since they returned from Lord Colville's ball hours ago.

Though admittedly, the gushing didn't help.

"He's so handsome, as well!" Harriett let out a sigh. "Have you ever seen a more handsome gentleman than Lord Wyle, Tilly?"

Had she? No one came to mind. No, she couldn't think of a single gentleman more handsome than Lord Wyle. He had those lovely dark eyes, after all. Deep, velvety dark eyes that put one in mind of the richest chocolate—

No, wait. Lord Wyle had blue eyes, didn't he? The velvety dark eyes belonged to—

Why, no one. No one at all. No one worth giving a

second thought, at any rate, and so, she wouldn't. No, indeed. Not a single second thought. Only—

"Tilly? Don't you think Lord Wyle is exceptionally handsome?"

"Oh, yes, of course! One can't fault Lord Wyle's appearance."

"He's ever so gallant, as well. Why, I can't think of a single gentleman in London with more bewitching manners." Harriett paused, then asked, "You do think my brother will approve of Lord Wyle, do you not, Tilly?"

Was there a thread of anxiety in Harriett's voice? That seemed odd, given Lord Wyle was what every brother must want for a beloved sister. "I daresay Lord Fairmont will be—"

"Lord Wyle has such a keen eye for fashion, too!" Harriett rushed on, any trace of apprehension lost in a girlish sigh. "Did you notice how perfectly turned out he was this evening? He quite eclipsed every other gentleman at the ball, did he not?"

"He did, indeed. I've never seen a gentleman with such a...such a..." Tilly frowned at the dark ceiling above her. What had Lord Wyle been wearing this evening? For the life of her, she couldn't recall a single item of the man's clothing. "A gentleman with such a flawlessly starched cravat."

Heavens, what a perfectly ridiculous thing to say, but all she could come up with regarding Lord Wyle's dress this evening was a vague notion that he'd been dressed very much as every other gentleman had been.

But it wouldn't do to say so to Harriett, who'd only become more smitten with Lord Wyle as the first few weeks of the season had come to an end. As for his lordship, he appeared equally smitten with Harriett. Their courtship was blossoming right before the *ton*'s eyes, and would almost certainly culminate in a betrothal before the end of the season, if not sooner.

It was precisely what she'd hoped for Harriett, and yet somehow, she couldn't work up the proper enthusiasm. Something was niggling at her, like a pebble caught in her half boot, stabbing at her with every step. She couldn't put her finger on it, but her mind kept returning to that odd comment Kit had made tonight after she'd told him scandal seemed to chase the Templetons wherever they went.

Bad luck, he'd said in reply, but then he'd muttered something under his breath about the Prestwick family knowing all about bad luck. It had seemed a strange thing for him to say, as the one thing everyone in London seemed able to agree on was that the Earls of Prestwick did as they pleased, and never troubled themselves much about what anyone else thought about it. They were, more than any other aristocratic family she could name, utterly unapologetic about their wickedness.

Except Kit *had* seemed troubled. A dark shadow had passed over his face when he said it, and then he'd quickly changed the subject.

"Lord Prestwick said something odd this evening, Harriett."

"Lord Prestwick?"

Harriett sounded surprised, as if she'd never heard the name Prestwick in her life, but Tilly swallowed back her impatience. Ladies in love were selfish creatures, after all.

"Yes. It was just an offhand comment, something about the Prestwick family having a history of bad luck, but it struck me as odd."

"Oh, I daresay he's referring to the curse."

"*Curse?*" Tilly propped herself up on her elbows and peered at Harriett through the darkness. "What curse?"

"You've never heard of the Prestwick curse?"

"No, not a word." Heavens, how could she have missed something as fascinating as that?

"I daresay it's because you've never to London before. The gossips claim that an ancient curse shadows the Prestwick sons. The way I heard it told, some wicked medieval ancestor broke his promise to wed an innocent young lady he'd compromised, and the girl's grandmother laid a curse on him as punishment."

"What sort of curse?"

"The very worst sort! Every subsequent Prestwick son is fated to die in a duel until the Prestwick line is extinguished forever. Fantastical, is it not?"

"That's ridiculous!" But was it, though? Was it any more ridiculous than believing scandal was stalking the Templetons?

"Yes. I daresay it's all nonsense, though it must be said that quite a few Earls of Prestwick have met their ends at the edge of a blade or, more recently, with the strike of a pistol ball."

A curse, of all things. Why hadn't Lady Fosberry mentioned anything about this curse?

Hariett's coverlet rustled as she rolled over in her bed. "Goodness, I'm tired! Good night, Tilly."

Dear God, how could Harriett possibly fall asleep *now*? "Er, good night."

She fell back against the bed, her head spinning so wildly it threatened to fly off her—

Neck. Oh, dear. Not the best analogy, perhaps.

It couldn't possibly be true, of course. There was no such thing as ancient curses.

Although...well, the world was filled with unexplainable things, wasn't it? And really, didn't the truth of the thing matter far less than whether or not Kit believed it to be true? And what did Harriett mean by 'quite a few earls.' How many earls?

She lay on her back on her bed, one hand buried in the warm fur of Lucifer's neck, the other pressed over her eyes in an attempt to keep them closed, and invite sleep to take her.

No, it was no use. She couldn't sleep. Not a single wink, until she knew the whole of it.

She waited until Harriett's breathing turned deep and even, then crawled out from under the coverlet and slid from the bed, pausing to throw her cloak over her night rail before gathering Lucifer into her arms. "Come along, Lucifer, and attend to your business. It's been ages since you've been out."

And if Lucifer happened to run over to Prestwick Cottage, as he was inclined to do, well...there was nothing she could do but follow him, was there?

Lucifer let out a sleepy growl of protest, but she pressed her hand over his mouth. "Hush, you wicked thing. It's time to make yourself useful, for once."

Oh, but this was a dreadful idea. Of course, it was. If scandal truly was haunting the Templetons, she was tempting it with every step she took toward her bedchamber door. Yet she didn't return to bed, as she should have, but slipped out into the corridor, a squirming Lucifer tucked under her arm.

~

LUCIUS CAME FIRST, his toenails clicking against the floors as he wandered into Kit's study.

A dozen questions flew through his head as the dog came toward him, but they were all the wrong questions. He should have been asking how Lucius happened to be there, how he'd gotten past the closed front door, and what the dog wanted this time, but instead, only one question echoed in his mind, and it silenced every other.

Where was Tilly?

He didn't have long to wait. Soft footsteps approached the study door, and she appeared a moment later, the dim light from the hall sconces behind her liming her dark hair and the long, slender lines of her body.

A young lady in her night rail wandering into his home in the middle of the night should have been cause for more surprise than he felt. But they'd been here before, he and Tilly, and no matter how unlikely a thing was, once it happened once, it could happen again.

Or perhaps, just this once, instead of punishing him, fate was gifting him with the one thing he'd come to want more than any other. Because somehow, there was a part of him that had been expecting her.

It didn't make sense, that she should have crept so thoroughly under his defenses, that a lady he'd met only a month ago could have curled so tightly inside his chest and made a home for herself there.

But he no longer cared whether any of this made

sense. He cared only that she was here, and her gaze was on *him*.

Only him.

She drifted closer, the white hem of her night rail dragging silently over the carpet, and came to a stop in front of his desk, like a figment from one of his dreams come to life. "Tonight at the ball, you said something about bad luck following the Prestwicks."

"Yes."

"Were you referring to the curse?"

Ah, someone had told her, then. It was hardly surprising. The *ton* loved to repeat the rumor of the ancient curse that had chased his family from one century to the next. "Yes. I suppose you think I belong in Bedlam, entertaining such foolishness."

She cocked her head to the side, studying him. Her long, dark hair was bound in a thick braid that dangled down her back, but a few dark chestnut locks had slipped free, the loose waves drifting over her shoulders and curling around her flushed face. What would those wispy curls feel like against his fingertips? Would they be as soft as they looked?

"I don't think it's foolish at all, Kit. Have you forgotten what I said about my family attracting scandal?"

It wasn't what he'd expected her to say, but when had she ever done as he'd expected? He shook his head. "No. Not a word of it."

"It doesn't matter what I believe, in any case." She drew closer, and slipped into the chair across from his desk. "What matters is whether *you* do. Do you believe you're cursed to die in a duel?"

Did he? God, he didn't know. It was so far-fetched, he half-questioned his own sanity for giving it a second thought. "I didn't used to, but then..." He swallowed.

"Then your uncle was killed in a duel," she murmured.

"Yes." He'd meant to end it at that, but somehow his mouth was opening again, words tumbling out. "It happened at Primrose Hill, only a few miles south of here. He took a ball to the stomach. He made it back to Prestwick House, but died soon afterwards in his bedchamber."

She was quiet for a moment, then she murmured, "That's why you stay here, in the cottage, rather than in Prestwick House."

"Yes." He'd hardly breathed a word about his uncle's death to anyone, but now the words were tearing loose, as if they'd been there on the tip of his tongue all along, waiting for someone who'd listen.

Waiting for *her*.

"It wasn't...a good death." It was an absurd thing to say. Was any death a good one? But she remained quiet, waiting. "It was excruciating, and bloody, and... and he regretted his life, at the end. Regretted the wrongs he'd done, and the people he'd hurt. I don't..."

He didn't want to die as Freddy had, wishing he'd been a better man.

"The curse," she said, when he remained silent. "I understand it was meant as a punishment for the ruination of a young lady. A young lady who was compromised, and then abandoned."

"So the rumor goes, yes. I have no idea whether or not the story is true. It's said to have happened some five or six hundred years ago, but I don't see why my distant ancestors should have been any different than the more recent crop of Prestwick earls."

"Kit." Her voice was gentle. "You can't mean to say you think you *deserve* to be cursed."

Did he think that? "Not exactly, but—"

"I know you're meant to be very wicked." She gave him a faint smile. "But I don't recall having heard that you've compromised and then abandoned any innocent young ladies."

He'd done any number of other wicked things—gaming, drinking, dallying with ladies of the demimonde and the occasional widow or bored wife. He was no pillar of ethical behavior by any means, but he'd never ruined an innocent.

Not until Tilly.

He rose from his chair, rounded the desk and came toward her, one slow, deliberate step at a time until he was so close he could inhale her scent of fresh air and gardens, and a hint of lavender soap. Heat curled inside him, a pulsing beat low in his belly.

She gasped when he knelt before her. "Kit?"

"You're wrong, Tilly. I *did* compromise a young lady. A lady with beautiful blue eyes who, by some mysterious stroke of fate came into my garden at night, just when I needed her the most."

She gazed at him, her eyes a dark blue in the flickering firelight. "You never...you didn't compromise me."

"But I did, Tilly. In the eyes of the *ton*, I did. We were here alone, and I kissed you." He reached for her, cupping her soft cheek in his palm. "Don't you remember?"

She didn't answer, but she did remember the kiss,

every moment of it. He saw it in the way her lips parted, and felt it in the shiver that went through her.

"I compromised you." He dragged his thumb over her cheekbone. "But I won't abandon you, Tilly."

She sucked in a quick breath. "You can't mean—"

"That I want you as my countess? That is what I mean. I want it more than anything."

"B-because of the curse?"

He wouldn't lie to her. "It began that way, yes, but it's no longer just about the curse. It's...you're..." God, his hands were shaking. "You're not like any lady I've ever met, Tilly. You're honest, and brave, and you make me wish I were a better man."

It wasn't a declaration of love—not quite—but it was as close as he'd ever come to one.

She looked down, but he caught her chin, and raised her face to his. "Why did you come here tonight, Tilly?"

"I don't... I shouldn't have."

"It's not too late to go." His hand fell away from her face. He wouldn't try and stop her if she fled. He'd let her go, and pretend he hadn't seen the desire in the midnight depths of her eyes, a desire that both thrilled and terrified him at once.

But that wasn't what she did.

She must know, just as he did, that this moment between them was inevitable. It had been bearing down on them since their first stolen kiss on the night they'd met.

And you couldn't outrun fate.

She stayed where she was, her gaze holding his. His heart thrashed madly in his chest, because he was going to kiss her, and she was... dear God, she was going to let him, was trembling for him as the moment unfolded between them.

One second passed, then another, her warm breath drifting against his cheek, and every inch of her quivering as she waited for his touch.

But he didn't kiss her mouth, Instead, he pressed his lips to her ear. "Why did you come here, Tilly?" he rasped.

"I wanted..."

"Yes?" He grazed her earlobe with the tip of his tongue, warmth exploding in his belly in a thousand bright sparks when she shivered against him. "What do you want?"

She put her palm on his chest. She was trembling, but she didn't push him away. She let her hand linger there, and he counted his heartbeats as the silence stretched between them.

"You," she whispered at last. "I want *you*."

He froze for an instant, then he let out a long, slow sigh. "If I were the man I should be, I'd send you away, but I can't, Tilly. I want you too much."

He kissed her then, his mouth taking hers, teasing at the seam of her lips with the tip of his tongue until she opened for him with a gasp. He plunged inside, groaning as she met him stroke for stoke, dizzy from the slick caress of her lips. "So good, Tilly. So sweet."

She didn't speak, only clung to him as desire surged between them, her head falling back as a helpless moan tumbled from her lips. Her fingers curled against his chest, fisting his linen shirt. "Oh, please."

He let out another low groan, and his hands slid to the small of her back, drawing her to the edge of the chair until she was nearly in his lap, every ragged breath she took echoing in his lungs. "Please, what? What do you want, Tilly?"

She didn't answer—not with words. Instead, she sank her fingers into his hair, and pulled his head down to hers.

CHAPTER
TWELVE

S he was the sweetest thing he'd ever tasted.

He slanted his mouth over hers, the hot rush of blood through his veins roaring in his ears, drowning out the faint voice reminding him she was an innocent.

An *innocent*, and so trusting, with big blue eyes a man could drown in.

And he was drowning, descending deeper with every gasp, every sigh and quiet moan, every shared breath between them. He wanted her so badly, was another brush of her lips away from gathering her into his arms, laying her down on his desk, and savoring her breathless cries as he took her, and made her his.

Do you think you deserve to be cursed?

How had she known to ask that question? No one had ever bothered to before. The truth...well, it shocked him, because he'd lived with the threat of the curse for so long, at some point, he'd begun to believe he *did* deserve it.

But did he? He wasn't as good a man as he ought to be— as he *could* be —but he wasn't like Freddy, or the other Earls of Prestwick who'd come before him. He'd never ruined an innocent. He'd never taken a young lady's virtue.

He'd never even been tempted.

Until now.

Tilly was an *innocent*.

But a need unlike any he'd never known had him in its grip, and it was hurtling him from one dizzying kiss to the next, the wild tide of desire sweeping everything else before it, and he was helpless to free himself from it.

He didn't *want* to be free of it. Not ever.

He was starved for her—for her mouth, her every breath, for the slender curves hidden underneath the night rail fisted in his hand. Every urge, every instinct screamed at him to lose himself in her, to let himself drown in an ocean of thick chestnut hair and soft, creamy skin.

"Kit." She twined her arms around his neck, and slid her fingers into his hair, dragging his head closer to hers, the soft stroke of her tongue inside his mouth stealing his breath, his reason. "Please."

Dear God, that soft plea went straight to his cock. He gasped when she met his frantic strokes, losing himself in the damp silk of her mouth, the shy caresses of her tongue against his, sweet, slick and devastating.

He had to slow down, to take a breath, and regain his wits.

"Tilly." He tore his mouth from hers, sucking a breath of air into his lungs, a rush of heady triumph roaring through him when she melted against him with a soft sigh, tucking her face against his neck.

His breath caught. It was so unexpected, that gesture, so *trusting*. What had he ever said or done to deserve her trust? The sweetness of it stunned him, swelling inside his chest, and twining around his heart.

He slid his palm from her neck to her chin, tilting her face up to his. Her mouth had gone a dark, wet pink from his kisses, and he leaned closer to nip at her swollen lower lip. Her fingers tightened in his hair, a needy sound falling from her lips.

"Shhh." He soothed the bite with gentle kisses to her lips, her cheek, his hand sliding lower to stroke the silky skin at the base of her neck, smiling at the frantic flutter of her pulse against his fingertips. Her breathing quickened at the light caress, and he urged her closer, desperate to feel the press of her body against his.

He wanted to touch her forever, learn every inch of her, make her sigh and gasp and beg with every stroke of his fingers, his tongue. He wanted to hold her against him, feel her shiver with pleasure. "You're so lovely, Tilly."

His lips followed the path his fingers had taken, dropping a dozen kisses along her neck and throat before moving back up to nibble on the sensitive skin behind her ear—she was so soft there, so warm—and taste the flutter of her pulse.

"Beautiful," he murmured, his other hand inching up her rib cage, dragging against the loose linen of her night rail. He reached out to trace his fingertip over the outline of her breast, lingering at the place where the neckline gave way to her skin. The firelight played over her, revealing teasing glimpses of the shadows of her nipples, and the perfect creamy swells of her breasts.

"Touch me, Kit." She caught his wrist, and placed his hand on her breast, gasping when he cupped her tenderly in his palm, his thumb brushing the straining peak of her nipple.

"Does it feel good when I touch you here?" he whispered, taking her mouth in another heated kiss as he teased the hardened nub, stroking her there until she was trembling in his arms, soft, desperate whimpers falling from her lips.

"I want your hands on me." He pressed one of her hands inside the open neck of his shirt, a low groan tearing from his throat when her fingers brushed his bare skin.

Dear God, what was she doing to him? He'd kissed many women, had touched them, but not one of them had ever maddened him the way she did. He wanted more, wanted her closer...

"Come here, love." He wrapped his hands around her waist, eased her onto her back against the soft carpet, then lowered himself on top of her, taking care to take his weight onto his arms so as not to crush her.

He was hard— God, had he ever been this hard? There was no way she couldn't feel the insistent length of him pressing into her belly. It was too much, too soon. She was an innocent, and he wouldn't frighten her for the world.

He let out a ragged sigh, and pressed his face into the silky arch of her neck, but when he began to shift away from her, she twined one leg around the back of his thigh, stopping him. "No. Don't go."

"Do you want me, Tilly?" If she did, then nothing in the world would tear him from her arms. Not her innocence, not the curse—nothing—because if she wanted him as much as he wanted her, then she would be his.

His.

"Yes." She dropped her forehead to his chest, her cheeks pink. "Yes, I want you."

"Then I won't leave you." He toyed with the edges of her cloak. "May I take this off?"

She gazed up at him, the firelight flickering over her delicate features, the blue eyes he'd begun to dream about fixed on his face, wide and trusting. "Yes."

He made quick work of the cloak, then settled back over her, pressing tender kisses to her forehead, her cheeks, her lips before sliding lower to taste the fragrant skin of her throat, and dear God, he wanted to taste her everywhere, to caress every inch of her skin with his lips, to devour her until she was writhing beneath him, begging him for the pleasure only he could give her, a pleasure she had no words for.

He trailed one hot kiss after another from her neck to the base of her throat, lingering over every kiss until at last—God, at last—he flicked his tongue over the tip of the blush pink nipple visible under the damp muslin of her night rail. She was sweet, so sweet, and so beautiful, with her hair a wild tangle around her face, and her nipples straining. "Does that feel good, love?"

"*Ah.*" She surged beneath him as he teased his tongue lightly over one hungry peak, her soft whimpers and the frantic tug of her hands in his hair driving him mad. "More. Please, Kit."

"I will never deny you anything, Tilly." He dropped a soft kiss between her breasts, then closed his lips around her engorged nipple, and suckled her through the muslin.

"Oh, oh..." Her head fell back against the carpet, her neck arching as he feasted on her, suckling and stroking one nipple, tugging the peak between his lips and caressing her with his tongue while he toyed with the other, pinching it gently between his fingers, dragging one helpless moan after another from her lips.

"That's it, love. Cry out for me," he whispered, his breath hot against her ear.

"I—I need..." Her words were drowned in another moan as he tugged her earlobe between his teeth, biting gently.

He knew what she needed, and there was nothing in the world that could have stopped him from giving it to her. "Open for me, Tilly," he murmured, pressing his palm against the inside of her thigh.

She didn't hesitate, but spread her legs for him at once. He held her gently, keeping her open to him as he slid his thigh between hers. "Does it ache here, Tilly?" He brushed his fingers over the soft, damp curls between her legs.

"Yes." Her hips jerked, straining against him. "Yes!"

He touched her again, letting his knuckles graze the sweet, tender nub there. "May I touch you?"

"Yes! *Please*, Kit."

Her soft, desperate pleas were driving him mad, driving him to abandon his intention to bring her to release with his fingers. The sweetness of her flesh, the slick honey...he had to taste her, couldn't go another moment without tasting her. He opened his mouth over the silky skin of her belly, then slid lower, lower, to the tender, aching nub between her thighs.

Closer, closer—

"Kit!" Tilly cried out when he pressed his lips to the inside of her thigh, and she surged upward, tugging at his hair, the furious flush in her cheeks visible even in the dim light. "You can't—"

"I can. I must." He eased her back down and pressed his palms against her thighs, holding her firmly open to him. "It's alright, love." He dipped down, and dropped a kiss on the secret place between her legs. "I just want to taste you. I have to taste you. Please, Tilly."

She said nothing, but slowly the tension in her body eased. Her fingers went limp in his hair, and then he was *there*, his tongue probing until a soft cry broke from her lips, and her knees fell open in silent invitation.

That was all he needed.

He stroked her with his tongue, lashing at the tiny bud between her silky thighs, over and over again until whatever misgivings she might have had about this most intimate of acts dissolved in another strangled moan. "Dear God, *Kit*."

"So sweet, Tilly." He growled against her quivering flesh. "So beautiful."

He couldn't get enough of her—the taste of her, delicate against his tongue, and her sounds, desperate moans and gasps as he licked and nipped at her slick flesh, drawing teasing circles with his tongue until she was clutching wildly at him, her hips surging higher with every caress, arching up to meet his mouth. "Please. Oh, please, Kit."

Did she know what she begging for?

It didn't matter. It didn't *matter*, because he knew, and he'd give it to her.

He'd give her everything.

"That's it, Tilly. Take your pleasure." He pressed her thighs open wider, caressing her with a few quick, light flicks of his tongue before he gave up his teasing, and stroked her harder, plunging between her swollen folds and suckling at her, his mouth moving desperately against her wet flesh. "Come for me."

She thrashed underneath him. "Yes. *Yes.*"

Her hips jerked, rising up to meet his strokes, and he gave her no quarter, but worked her ruthlessly, relentlessly, driving her higher with every stroke, her tender bud swelling against his insatiable tongue, until at last a sharp cry broke from her lips, and she shuddered against him, her back arching with her release.

He stayed with her, his lips gentling as she rode the waves of bliss until she went limp, and fell back against the rug, gasping. He wrapped his arms around her hips then, pressing a kiss to her thigh before resting his head against her belly, nuzzling her soft skin as she caught her breath.

"Are you...was that...are you alright?" God above, he sounded like a schoolboy with his first woman, but he had to know, had to hear from her lips that he hadn't frightened her, that he'd given her pleasure.

She didn't answer at once, and dread rolled over him. Had he pushed her too hard? She was an *innocent*, and he'd just—

"Kit?"

He froze, squeezing his eyes closed. "Yes?"

She sank her fingers into his hair, toying with the

strands for a moment before giving it a gentle tug. "Come here."

She didn't *sound* frightened, but his heart was pounding in his chest as he shifted up and over her. She was still, one arm flung over her head, her heavy eyes mysterious pools of darkness. Her cheeks were flushed, and a fine sheen of perspiration had bloomed on her skin. He'd never seen anything more beautiful than she was as she lay there, trembling with the aftershocks.

"Closer, Kit." She reached for him, her face aglow with the flush of her release, and a dreamy smile curving her lips. "Closer."

He own lips curved in what was no doubt an absurdly besotted smile before he stretched out beside her, wrapped his arm around her waist, and gathered her close against him. "Alright?" he murmured, curling a lock of her hair around his finger.

She let out a long, slow sigh, and rested her cheek against his chest. "Perfect."

∼

THE ROOM WAS QUIET, the only sound the faint crackling of the fire in the grate. Tilly slumped against Kit, her entire body limp. Had she ever felt this boneless before? No, but then she'd never before experienced the pleasure he'd given her.

His arm was curled tightly around her, his chest moving under her cheek in slow, even breaths, but he didn't speak. She tilted her head back to look at him, and she found him watching her, his lids gone heavy over his dark eyes.

He hadn't asked her to touch him. He hadn't

asked her for anything at all, but she could feel his, er...that is, the most intimate part of him pressing hard against her thigh.

It couldn't be pleasant for a gentleman, leaving such an insistent organ as that unsatisfied. How one might satisfy such an organ was a mystery to her, but it didn't seem right to leave him in such a state, when he'd attended so generously to her pleasure.

In any case, she was curious.

She stroked her thumb against the bare, warm skin of his neck, then slowly, tentatively let her hand drift lower, her palm skimming over his chest and down his torso to his lower belly—

"*Tilly.*" He caught her wrist, holding her still, even as his hips thrust upward helplessly, as if seeking her touch. "What are you doing?"

"Touching you?" She peered up at him, at his handsome face, lost in shadows. "Should I not?"

He let out a strained laugh. "I shouldn't let you."

"That's not what I asked, Lord Prestwick." She levered up onto her elbow, pressed a kiss to his jaw, then settled back down beside him, and let her hands wander over his muscular body. Soon enough he was shuddering, as if it were taking every bit of his restraint not to leap upon her.

Dear God, it was heady, having such a powerful man so hungry for her touch that he couldn't keep still. But some of her bravado fled at the sight of his cock twitching insistently against his falls. "I'm not, er...exactly sure how to do this."

"Like this." He loosened his falls, then took one of her hands, guided it to his stiff cock, and showed her how to stroke him. "That's it. God, *yes*," he hissed, closing his eyes and arching his back. "Just like that, Tilly."

A shiver tripped down her spine at the low rasp of his voice. She leaned closer to study his engorged cock, the tip red and straining against his stomach, fascinated. She slid her hand down his hard length slowly, taking care not to squeeze too hard, and savoring the slide of the loose, warm skin over the hard length beneath.

"*Yes*, Tilly. A little harder." He gave one quick, involuntary thrust beneath her before he stilled, but he couldn't hide his panting breaths as she continued her caresses, his skin dampening and his neck muscles cording with the effort of staying still.

It was wicked, the surge of desire that rushed through her at his struggle; wicked, the surge of heat between her legs as she he writhed and groaned under her seeking hand. She'd never given a man pleasure before, and she'd never imagined it could be so breathlessly exciting. "Is this alright?" She swiped her thumb over the moisture that had gathered at his tip. "May I touch you here?"

"God, yes." He gasped, his hips jerking.

"Are you...can you..." Could he reach his pleasure like this, with just her touch?

"*Yes*." His hips rose, moving in rhythm with her steady strokes. "Don't stop. Please, Tilly. You're going to make me—*ah*." He cried out, his cock jerking in her hand as his release took him, hot seed shooting from his tip, coating her hand and his stomach. He thrust into her fist—once, and then again—a harsh groan falling from his lips, his powerful body shuddering until the spasms passed, and he fell back, limp.

She gazed down at him as his breathing slowed.

He didn't say a word, but his sleepy dark eyes, the warmth in them as he gazed back up at her seemed to say a thousand words at once.

She reached down, brushing away a lock of his auburn hair that had fallen into his eyes, and he caught her hand, and pressed a kiss to her palm. Her breath caught, and a rush of tears blurred her eyes at the tender gesture, and the softness in his face as he looked up at her.

It was silly to cry.

So she buried her face in the arch between his neck and shoulder to hide her tears, her heart beating in a wild rhythm in her chest.

She didn't regret what they'd done. How could she?

But this was nothing like their first meeting. It wasn't an accidental kiss between two strangers. Nor was it an innocent stroll at a picnic, or a dance at a ball, or even a secret matchmaking scheme, as scandalous as that was.

There was no going back from *this*.

In the space of a few delirious hours, everything had changed.

CHAPTER
THIRTEEN

It was difficult to say how much time passed as they lay there entwined in each other's arms. Perhaps it was an hour or more, but it seemed as if only a few precious moments had passed before Tilly noticed the first glimmers of light in the sky.

It was dark still, but morning was coming.

"I have to go." She slipped out of Kit's embrace, every part of her howling in protest at the loss of his heat, the strong, steady beat of his heart against her cheek, the strength of his arms around her, but it was tempting fate, remaining here any longer.

Kit let out a grumble of protest, and before she could rise, she'd been tumbled backwards against a muscular chest, and a bristly jaw was nuzzling her throat. "No. Not yet."

Oh, if only she could stay! If only the sun would hold off a few moments longer! It was still several hours until Lady Fosberry's household would begin to awaken, but if Harriett should happen to notice her bed was empty, or if Phee came in search of her, as she sometimes did in the mornings.... no. It was madness to risk it.

"I must, Kit. I've been here too long already."
She wriggled loose from his arms, and stumbled
to her feet. Her night rail was a crumpled mess,
and her hair had come loose from her braid and
was tumbled down her back in a riot of tangled
curls, but there was no time to search for hair-
pins. She'd just have to pray no one saw her
creeping away from Prestwick Cottage, looking as
if she'd been...well, as if she'd been doing precisely what she *had* been doing with the Earl of
Prestwick.

Kit sighed, but he rose and retrieved her cloak
from the floor. "Come here."

She did as he bid, and stood obediently still while
he draped the cloak over her shoulders, but she
couldn't bring herself to look him in the eye after
what she—what *they*—had done.

Dear God, what had ever possessed her to behave
like such a wanton? She bit her lip, heat scalding her
cheeks. He'd put his *mouth* on her, between her, er...
and she—well, she was no better! She'd touched his...
caressed it, until he'd—

"Such a fetching blush, Tilly." Kit brushed a
knuckle across her cheekbone. "Such a pretty pink."
He traced the wash of heat down her neck to the
hollow of her throat, his dark eyes gleaming as his
gaze followed the path his hand had taken. "How far
down does it go?"

All the way.

He let out a soft laugh, and she peeked up to find
him gazing down at her, a wicked grin on his lips. But
his eyes were aglow with the same sweetness she'd
noticed the first time she'd ever looked into them.
She'd thought him a drunkard and a scoundrel that

night, but even then, she'd admired his eyes, so dark and warm, like melted chocolate.

"It's chilly." One by one, he fastened the buttons of her cloak, then tied the ribbon in a bow at her neck. It was a tender gesture, and once again foolish tears stung her eyes. A few kisses and sweet whispers, and she'd turned into a watering pot. Why, she was no better than all the other young ladies who'd gone crazy over the handsome Earl of Prestwick the moment he appeared at the first ball of the season.

"There." He draped the deep, woolen hood over her head, then plucked up his own coat from the arm of a chair. "Now we can go."

"We? You can't come with me! What if someone sees us?" All it would take was one gossiping neighbor glancing out their window at the wrong time— a breath of rumor whispered into a willing ear — and the scandal would spread like a conflagration.

"I'm coming with you, Tilly. I won't send you out into the dark alone."

She opened her mouth to remind him she'd come to the cottage alone in the dark, but his jaw had gone tight, and there didn't seem any point in arguing with him. "Yes, alright, but only as far as Lady Fosberry's garden gate."

"Stubborn chit." He reached out and tweaked one of her loose curls. "Very well."

"Thank you. Now, what do you suppose has become of Lucifer? Oh, there he is." Instead of vanishing into the depths of the cottage like the imp he was, Lucifer had curled up on a plump settee near the fire, and gone to sleep.

He let out a sleepy grunt when she gathered him into her arms, but he allowed himself to be wrapped in the loose folds of her cloak, and carried out the door and into the garden. It *was* chilly, just as Kit had said, the ground covered with a thin layer of frost that crunched beneath their feet as they made their way across the pathway to the wrought iron fence.

It was silly of her, but a sudden bashfulness overcame her when they paused by the gate, and she peeked up at him to find him gazing down at her, his face half lost in shadows, and the other half limned in silver moonlight.

What was happening to her? She wasn't some bashful maiden who couldn't meet a man's gaze without blushing. But then, had there ever been a man who looked more beautiful in the moonlight than he, with his tousled auburn hair, and the shadow of dark bristles sprouting on his strong jaw?

It had been wrong of her to kiss him. Wrong to touch him, and to do all the other risky and wonderful things she'd done with him, but even now, standing in a wind so chill it should have brought her to her senses, her heart was free of regret.

There was no telling what would happen between them now. Perhaps they'd behave as they'd done before tonight, as if they scarcely knew each other. He might go on to marry Lady Anne Wilmot, or Lady Cressida, and she'd return to Hambleden with Phee and resume her quiet life.

But never— *never* —would she ever wish to undo those magical moments with him. At night, when she was alone in her bed, she'd think of him, and hold the memory of his kiss close to her heart.

She peeked up at him from under her lashes. "Goodnight."

"Goodnight?" He drew closer, a smile tugging at his lips. "Is that all, Tilly?"

"Well, I..." She trailed off with a swallow as he cupped her cheeks in his hands, his palms impossibly warm against her skin, and in the next breath he was kissing her, his warm lips and the moonlight caressing her face luring her into a thousand romantic dreams.

It wasn't a carnal kiss—not the delirious conquering of her mouth that made her nerve endings leap to life and clamor for more—but a sweet, gentle kiss, his tongue daring only a brief foray between her lips before he set her away from him with a groan. "Go, Tilly, before I snatch you up and take you back to the cottage with me." He brushed his thumb over her lower lip. "I'll come to you tomorrow."

She nodded, then forced herself to take a step backwards, then another, then she turned and fled before she could give in to the wild urgings of her heart, and throw herself back into his arms.

Lucifer poked his head out from the folds of her cloak as she stumbled through the gate and ran through the rose garden to the south side of the lawn, where she might sneak through the door that led to the kitchen and up the back staircase. Just a little further, and she'd be safely tucked into her bed, and no one any the wiser—

"Grrr."

"Lucifer?" She paused on one side of the tall hedge that separated the garden from a narrow drive that led to the kitchens. Lucifer's small body had gone stiff against her, and his chest vibrated with another growl. "Whatever is the matter?"

Had someone seen them? She glanced around, her

ANNA BRADLEY

heart thumping, but this part of the lawn was secluded, hidden on one side by the tall oaks that lined
the front drive, and the thick hedge on the other, and
there didn't seem to be anyone about. "Hush, Lucifer.
There's no one here."

But the words had scarcely left her lips before she
heard it, the faint but unmistakable jingle of a har-
ness, then a horse's snort, coming from the other side
of the hedge. She clutched Lucifer to her chest. Why
in the world would someone be riding a horse *here*, at
this time of—

"...break my family's heart."

Dear God, there were voices, coming from the
other side of the hedge! She crept closer and peeked
through a gap in the branches. On the other side,
parked in the drive was a black, unmarked carriage.

"You would break my heart instead?" a man
replied, his tone low and urgent.

She sucked in a stunned breath. Two dark figures
stood before the carriage. She couldn't see their faces
—the moon was such that she could only see their
silhouettes—but she would have known the woman
anywhere.

Harriett, it seemed, had secrets of her own.

Because it *was* Harriett, and beside her stood a
much taller, broader figure, and he was speaking
earnestly to her, his words rapid. There was nothing
threatening in his tone, but his large body was tense
in a way that made the hairs on Tilly's arms rise in
alarm.

What in the world was Harriett *doing*, meeting a
gentleman in the kitchen drive at night?

Except she knew already, didn't she? What
reason could there be for a young lady to meet a

man alone at night—a man in an unmarked carriage, at that—unless she were absconding with him?

The man must be Lord Wyle. Harriett would never agree to such a disgraceful scheme for any other gentleman, but she fancied herself madly in love with Lord Wyle, and goodness knew there wasn't a creature alive more foolish than a lady in love.

But dear God, an elopement? Why in the world should Lord Wyle wish for such a thing? He was the Nonesuch, for pity's sake, the gentleman every young lady in London wanted! He was handsome, wealthy, and titled. What reason could he have for absconding with his bride?

"I can't stop thinking of my poor Aunt, who's been so kind to me." Harriett sounded as if she were near tears. "And my brother! He'll never forgive—"

Lord Wyle cut her off. "Don't be ridiculous, Harriett. No brother could be anything other than thrilled to see his sister become the Countess of Wyle."

"Why can't we wait until James arrives in London? He's certain to approve the match—"

"I already told you why, Harriett." Lord Wyle sounded as if he were endeavoring to be patient, but there was a harsh edge to his voice. He'd moved closer to Harriett, and was crowding her against the carriage.

Tilly froze, the cold, dark note in his voice chilling her from head to toe. There was something terribly wrong here. Terribly, horribly wrong. Lord Wyle was not the gentleman everyone in London believed him to be.

Harriett was teetering on the edge of a catastrophic misstep. She had to put a stop to this at once, before—

"...a dreadful mistake." Harriett's voice was shaking. "It was wrong of me to agree to it. Very wrong, indeed. I beg your pardon, Edward, but I can't go through with this."

She'd been endeavoring to skirt around Lord Wyle as she spoke, but his hand shot out, and he grabbed her arm. "You can, Harriett, and you *will*."

Dear God, he was going to force Harriett into the carriage!

Tilly's blood froze in her veins at the thought, her every instinct urging her to charge into the drive, leap upon Lord Wyle, and demand he release Harriett at once. But mightn't he be able to overpower them both? He was quite a big man, and he...wasn't he holding something in his hand?

She peeked through the hedge again, her heart vaulting into her throat.

He had a crop. All it would take was one flick of his wrist to stop her. She could scream, and call every servant inside the house down upon them, but the kitchen window was dark, and the bedchambers were on the other side of the house. She might scream herself hoarse without anyone hearing her.

"Quickly, Lucifer." She pressed her face into the dog's fur, hoping against hope that he understood her, and just this once, would do as she bid him. "Go and fetch Kit." She set Lucifer on his feet. He didn't hesitate, but tore off in a cloud of white fur, his small paws barely skimming the ground. "Yes, that's it, Lucifer. *Run.*"

There was no time to wait and see if he went in the direction of the cottage—no time even for a muttered prayer before Harriett let out a sharp cry, her voice trembling with fear. "Let go of me!"

There was no time for anything but to fly through the opening in the hedge.

In an instant, she'd tumbled into the drive. "Harriett!"

The two figures froze.

"Tilly!" Harriett cried, but her voice was drowned out by the curses falling from Lord Wyle's lips. "Hell, and damnation. Where the devil did you come from?"

Harriett was struggling in earnest now, scratching and fighting like a wildcat to get free of Lord Wyle's grip, but it was clear she was no match for his strength. She let out a cry of pain as he wrenched her arm behind her back. "Enough, damn you!"

"Lord Wyle!" Tilly rushed forward, stunned to find her legs were still working. "Lady Harriett has demanded that you release her *at once!*"

"Lady Harriett isn't in a position to demand anything." Lord Wyle had his arms locked around Harriet now, and was dragging her toward the open door of the carriage. "Neither, Miss Mathilda, are you. Stay back, or you'll regret it!" He added, brandishing the crop.

Harriett fought him, but it was no use. He dragged her along the drive as if she weighed no more than a reticule, one inexorable step after another until he reached the carriage. He shoved her inside, slammed the door behind her, and hurried toward the driver's box.

Oh, what was she going to do? She couldn't let him take Harriett, but by time she fetched a servant and they made it back to the drive, Lord Wyle and

Harriett would be gone. Then there'd be a chase, and a most spectacular scandal would follow, and poor Harriett's tender heart would be broken, just as Phee's had been six years earlier.

But she could leap upon him just as he was ascending the box, and pray that the awkwardness of his position would make him lose his balance long enough for her to get Harriett out of the carriage, and into the house.

There was really only one choice.

She rushed forward, and leapt.

CHAPTER
FOURTEEN

K it had just banked the fire in his study and was making his way upstairs to his bed-chamber, his head filled with memories of Tilly's kisses when he heard a strange scratching at the front door.

He rushed back down the stairs and threw it open, hoping Tilly had returned, but it wasn't Tilly he found waiting for him on the other side.

It was Lucius. His white fur was mussed, and he was panting heavily, his tongue hanging out of his mouth. "Did you run away from Tilly again? Bad dog, Lucius."

Lucius darted down the steps, but he didn't vanish into the garden. Instead he turned back, letting out a loud "Woof!" when Kit didn't follow.

Something was wrong. Something had happened to Tilly.

He didn't stop to think, or even to draw a breath before he was out the door and down the steps, Lucius flying before him, a dozen different nightmare scenarios playing through his head as he ran—Tilly lying on the cold ground, one of her limbs twisted from a fall, or Lady Fosberry's house enveloped in flames.

But when he reached the gate that enclosed her ladyship's rose garden, there was no fire, and no sign of Tilly. The garden was deserted. He stilled, listening, but aside from his own harsh breaths sawing in and out of his lungs, all was silent, and the garden gate where he'd kissed Tilly not half an hour earlier was closed and latched. "Where is she, Lucius?"

The dog whined, pawing at the ground near the closed gate. Kit fumbled at the latch with clumsy fingers, but at last he managed to wrench it open. "Take me to her, Lucius."

Lucius darted though the open gate, his tiny paws scrambling beneath him as he tore across the garden in the direction of the front drive. But it was deserted as well, and the house was still and silent, without so much as a flicker of candlelight in any of the windows. With the silvery rays of moonlight shining down on it, it looked like the very picture of calm peacefulness.

If it hadn't been for Lucius, Kit might have believed all was as peaceful as it appeared, but the uneasiness in his chest told him it was an illusion. Something was terribly wrong. He could sense it now, the prickling at the back of his neck growing more pronounced as he and Lucius drew closer to the house.

The dog bypassed the front drive without a pause, and scurried toward the edge of the lawn, a blurry ball of white fur rolling across the lawn like a billiards ball over the baize, leaving a trail of tiny pawprints in his wake.

Kit tore after him, his lungs burning, the crunch of

his footsteps against the frosted ground echoing in his ears, and God, he'd been running for hours trying to get to her, the lawn unfolding in an endless ribbon of green under his feet until at last—*at last*—he ground to a halt.

Lucius had come to a dead stop at the hedge. He turned his face up to Kit, but there was no urgent barking this time, no whining. He was strangely quiet, as if listening for something.

Kit sucked in a breath, and held it.

That was when he heard it. It was faint, but it sounded like....yes, it was!

On the other side of the hedge, a lady was weeping. No, she was *sobbing*, the desperate sobs of someone so panicked they were unable to catch their breath.

Was it Tilly? He stilled, straining to hear, but didn't one lady's sobs sound very much like another's?

No, as it happened, because somehow, he knew at once it wasn't Tilly who was sobbing, but another lady. Who? Lady Harriett, perhaps, but then where was Tilly? What had become of her?

He couldn't see a damned thing with the bloody hedge in the way—

"Lord Wyle! Lady Harriett has demanded you release her at once!"

Tilly! It was her. There was no mistaking her voice.

"Lady Harriett isn't in a position to demand anything, and neither, Miss Mathilda, are you!"

God above, was that *Wyle*? His voice was so harsh and menacing it was nearly unrecognizable, but it sounded like—

"Stay back, or you'll regret it!"

It *was* Wyle, and he was threatening Tilly.

Kit's vision blurred, and his hands curled into fists. He burst through a narrow gap in the hedge, the branches tearing at his clothing and leaving a long, wicked scratch on his cheek, and on the other side, in the center of the drive...

For an instant, he froze in shock. If he hadn't seen it himself, he never would have believed Wyle capable of such perfidy, but the truth of it was right before his eyes.

One of Wyle's arms was locked around Harriett's throat, the other around her waist, and he was dragging her—dragging a *lady*, the scoundrel—toward the open door of the carriage waiting in the drive. Tilly was following them, one cautious step at a time, the slender lines of her body rigid, a riding crop clutched in her fist.

She was afraid— he could feel her fear as if it were his own, the frenzied pounding of her heart as if it lived inside his own chest, but she never paused in her pursuit. She was going after Wyle, a man nearly three times her size, to save her friend.

Harriett was struggling against Wyle's hold, her anguished sobs growing louder with every step across the drive, but she may as well have been fighting against a bear, for all the effect it was having. Wyle was simply too large, and too strong. Within minutes he'd made it across the drive, and with one mighty heave, he tossed Lady Harriett into the carriage.

He ran for the box, but Tilly jumped into his way before he could reach it. "You're not taking Harriett, my lord," she warned, slicing the air with the crop as if it were a rapier.

"Oh, but I am." Wyle lunged for Tilly, his arms out in front of him and fingers curled into claws as if he were anticipating wrapping them around her neck.

But she was too quick for him, and leapt nimbly out of his reach. "Harriett isn't going anywhere with you, my lord. Someone inside the house is sure to have heard us by now. I'd go now, if I were you, while you still can."

"Ah, but you're not me, Miss Mathilda." He charged at her once again, and this time he managed to catch the end of the riding crop. He gave it a wicked wrench, twisting Tilly's arm. She cried out, her grip on the crop loosening. Wyle saw his chance, and jerked it out of her hand.

At the sound of Tilly's pained cry, the shock that had held Kit in a frozen fog dissolved, and a cold, dark fury unlike any he'd ever felt before descended on him, engulfing him in a haze of red.

As soon as the scoundrel raised his hand to Tilly, everything had become crystal clear.

Wyle had *hurt* her, and that had been a drastic mistake.

"Tilly!" Lady Harriett shrieked. She was in full hysterics now, her sobbing having given way to a wailing that would surely draw the servants from the house.

But there wasn't time to wait.

Wyle was advancing on Tilly, the crop raised to strike. She backed away from him, but after a few steps she stumbled, and fell onto her backside in the drive. Her eyes went wide and dark with fear as Wyle drew closer, his face scarlet, and a cascade of vile threats and curses pouring from his lips.

Kit didn't give him a chance to make good on them.

He didn't remember moving, but he must have done, because the next thing he knew he was in the drive, his body between Wyle and Tilly, blocking Wyle's advance. He was vaguely aware of Tilly scrambling to her feet behind him, and of Lucius barking, and the carriage door flying open, but he never took his eyes off Wyle. "Have I caught you at an awkward moment, Wyle?"

"This doesn't concern you, Prestwick," Wyle snarled. "Be on your way."

"No. I don't believe I will. I think I'll stay right where I am. Oh, and I'll be taking that crop, as well."

Wyle made another clumsy swipe with the crop. "I'll beat you bloody with it first, Prestwick."

"I doubt it. You would have done well to follow Miss Mathilda's advice, Wyle, and leave while you had the chance, because God knows you've made a mess of this. So much for being the Nonesuch, eh? But have it your way, if you must."

Wyle didn't waste any time. He took a wild swing at Kit's head, but he was far too furious to take proper aim, and the blow fell short. He jerked his arm back to attempt a second attack, but before he could gather his wits Kit slammed a fist into his face. Pain exploded across his knuckles, but there was a satisfying crack, and an instant later a fountain of blood spurted from Wyle's nose.

That should have been the end of it, but Wyle, maddened by pain and his disappointed hopes regarding Lady Harriett, came at Kit like a man possessed.

"Kit!" Tilly screamed, just as the crop sliced through the air in an arc, and came down hard on Kit's arm. Blood blossomed in the wake of the blow, soaking the arm of Kit's white linen shirt. It hurt like the devil, but he sucked in a sharp breath and shook off the pain. "Come, Wyle. You can do better than that."

Wyle charged forward, aiming another strike at Kit's jaw. Kit leapt backwards just in time, dodging the blow, and a good thing, because Wyle had thrown his weight behind the attack. If it had landed, it likely would have broken his jaw.

Alas for Wyle, he stumbled, the momentum from his furious attack carrying him forward, and Kit finished the job by sweeping his leg out from under him with a well-aimed kick.

Wyle fell heavily onto his side, his temple striking the ground. The crop fell from his hand, and bounced across the drive. In a flash, Tilly darted forward and snatched it out of Wyle's reach, but by then, the battle was already over.

Everyone could see it but Wyle, who staggered, but managed to regain his feet. He made a few half-hearted attempts to land a fist to Kit's rib cage, but he was panting with exhaustion, and looked half mad, with sweat and the blood from his broken nose streaming down his face.

Or more than half. He'd have to be mad, to make such a foolhardy attempt to make off with Lady Harriett against her will. It didn't make sense he should have resorted to this, when he'd spent all season successfully courting her.

Anyone could see Lady Harriett was in love with him, or had been, before Wyle revealed his violent nature. What had pushed him into such a desperate attempt?

There was more to this story, but Kit was in no frame of mind to hear it. Lady Harriett had fallen into hysterics, and was babbling incoherently to Tilly, who was attempting to soothe her, but Tilly's face was as pale as death, and the hand stroking Harriett's back was shaking.

All he wanted, all he could think of, was wrapping his arms around her, and cradling her head against his chest.

Wyle would be dealt with, but not now.

He stepped up to Wyle, his voice grim. "Get out of here."

For a moment, Wyle looked as if he were considering another attack. It was a sure sign he'd lost his wits entirely, as any sane man could see this was finished, but at that moment a lantern flared to life in an upstairs window of Fosberry House. A second lantern followed, the light casting a faint glow onto the drive.

"Lady Fosberry and her servants will be crowding the drive soon. I hate to think what she'll have her footmen to do you, Wyle, when she sees the state her niece is in."

Wyle turned back toward the carriage.

"Leave it. Just go, *now*."

Wyle cast him a glance of pure hatred, but he turned without a word, and limped toward the hedge.

"Oh, and Wyle?" Kit called.

Wyle turned.

"This isn't over."

Wyle didn't reply, but slunk through the gap in the hedge, and disappeared into the darkness.

Kit waited until he was sure Wyle was gone before rushing to Tilly.

Harriett had collapsed in a heap in the drive, having nearly sobbed herself into a swoon. Lucius had curled up in her lap, and she was stroking him, and listening to Tilly, who was murmuring to her.

"Shh, Harriett. It's alright, dearest. He's gone, and you're safe now."

"Tilly." Kit's voice was hoarse.

She whirled toward him. "Kit." She gazed at him for a moment, then without any hesitation she ran across the drive, and threw herself into his arms. "Thank God you came."

He closed his arms around her, and pulled her tightly against him. "I'll always come for you, Tilly. Always."

"I—I don't understand it, Kit. Why did he...how could he have done this?" She shook her head, the tears she'd held back during the ordeal filling her eyes.

He eased her face down to his chest and held her as she wept quietly, her tears dampening the front of his shirt. He would have kept her there all night, safe in his arms, but Tilly being the fierce lady she was, she recovered quickly. She pulled back a little so she could look up at him, and a distressed cry left her lips. "You're bleeding!"

He glanced down at his arm, where the blood was still oozing from the gash Wyle had given him. "It will heal."

"But your face!" She reached up to stroke his

cheek, a tear slipping free. "Did he catch you with the tip of the crop?"

"No, the hedge did that." He smiled down at her. "Why does Lady Fosberry permit such dangerous shrubbery on her grounds?"

Despite everything she'd been through tonight, the smile he'd come to adore blossomed on her lips. "I can't imagine. We'll have to have a word with her, won't we?"

Behind them, the kitchen door flew open, and a chorus of shouts could be heard coming from the house. "Ah. The servants are coming."

He should have let her go then—if she was seen in his arms, the tongues would start wagging—but he couldn't bear to let her go yet, and perhaps she felt the same, because she made no move to get free. They simply stood there together, and waited for the servants to arrive.

But the first person to reach them wasn't one of Lady Fosberry's servants.

It was Lord Fairmont.

CHAPTER
FIFTEEN

"Under the circumstances, I think we can dispense with the tea." Lady Fosberry strode directly from the drawing room door to the sideboard. She plucked up a bottle of sherry, then set it aside with a shake of her head, and snatched up a bottle of brandy, instead. "Tumblers, if you would, Watkins. Hurry, man."

The tension in the room was so thick Tilly could almost see it, swirling between them all like a poisonous fog, but Lord Fairmont had enough self-control to wait until Watkins left the drawing room before he exploded. "What the devil happened out there tonight, Prestwick?"

He was a handsome man, with dark hair and fine, classical features very much like Harriett's, but he would have been a great deal more handsome if his blue eyes hadn't been narrowed to slits, and his lips twisted into a fearsome frown.

One could hardly blame him, however, given the pitiful state Harriett had been in when he found her. The shock of Lord Wyle's attack, and the unexpected appearance of her brother after a six years absence had entirely overset her. She'd fallen into deep, gulping sobs that sounded as if they'd been torn from her very soul, and had to be dosed with laudanum, and taken directly to bed.

"Nothing to say, Prestwick? Very well, then I'll tell you what it looked like to me." Lord Fairmont had been pacing from one end of the drawing room to the other, but now he stopped in front of Kit, his eyes blazing with fury.

Why was he angry at Kit? He couldn't possibly think that—

"It looks as if *you*, a known rake and seducer, were attempting to abscond with my sister tonight!"

"James!" Lady Fosberry gasped.

"No!" Tilly cried at the same time, leaping to her feet. "You're mistaken, Lord Fairmont! That's not what happened—"

"Sit *down*, Tilly," Phee snapped. She grabbed Tilly's hand and gave it a sharp tug.

Tilly's knees buckled, and she collapsed onto the settee, blinking away the tears that rushed to her eyes. Phee had *never* spoken to her in such a harsh tone before, and it hit her like a blow. "Phee?"

Phee's face softened. "I beg your pardon, dearest, but this matter is between Lord Fairmont and Lord Prestwick, and you *will* let them speak."

Kit's jaw had gone tight at the accusation, but he met Lord Fairmont's gaze without flinching. "Someone attempted to abscond with Lady Harriett tonight, but it wasn't me, Fairmont. I came upon Lord Wyle trying to drag your sister into the carriage."

"Lord Wyle," Lord Fairmont repeated flatly. "That's curious, Prestwick, because I didn't see Lord Wyle there. I saw my sister in hysterics, an unmarked black carriage, and you, bloody and panting, and this young lady." He nodded at Tilly. "Whom I've never seen before in my life!"

Was Lord Fairmont accusing her of something, as well? She opened her mouth to defend herself, but Kit got there first. "This young lady is Miss Mathilda Templeton, and you owe her your thanks, Fairmont. If it weren't for her, Wyle would be on his way to Gretna Green with Lady Harriett by now."

"I don't understand how we could have so mistaken Lord Wyle's character!" Lady Fosberry interrupted, wringing her hands. "Why, I've never heard a single word against him, not even a breath of scandal about him! How could this have happened?"

"You can't mean to say you believe Prestwick, Aunt!" Lord Fairmont turned on Lady Fosberry, incredulous. "Lord Wyle is the Nonesuch, for God's sake, and Prestwick is a notorious rake! Imagine my shock when I returned to England to find the gentleman to whom I'd promised my sister had a list of scandals to his name longer than my arm!"

"I don't deny it." Kit's face had gone pale, but he remained calm, and met Lord Fairmont's gaze steadily. "But while I may be a rake, Fairmont, I'm not a despoiler of innocents, or a kidnapper."

"Very well, Prestwick. If it's as you say, then perhaps you'd care to explain what you were doing out on the drive at two o'clock in the morning, and pray, don't insult my intelligence by saying you just happened to be there."

A tense silence fell, and might have gone on for some time as they all squirmed in their seats, but Lady Fosberry broke it. "I'd like to know that, as well."

"As would I," Phee said. "I was under the impression, Tilly, that you were tucked safely into your bed. What were you doing outside in the drive in the middle of the night?"

Phee was utterly furious with her. There was no mistaking the anger, the disappointment in her eyes, yet she was still holding Tilly's hand, and she gave it a little squeeze now, as if to reassure her.

But Tilly didn't have a single reassuring word to offer her sister in return. She might have lied, and said Lucius had woken her, and she'd taken him out to do his business, but that wouldn't explain why Kit had been there, would it?

She opened her mouth, even as she had no idea on earth what to say, but once again, Kit saved her. "Lucius has taken to visiting the cottage recently, and he appeared on my doorstep tonight. I found Miss Mathilda in the rose garden when I brought him back. She'd taken him out, and he'd gotten away from her."

That was... well, yes, that would do, wouldn't it?

Phee had been as rigid as a fireplace poker beside her since they'd sat down, but at this explanation, some of the tension drained from her body. She believed Kit's story, then. That should have reassured Tilly, but somehow, it only made her feel worse.

How many times was she going to have to lie to her sister?

Phee deserved better than that. She deserved the truth.

She glanced down at her hands, her cheeks hot with shame, but her head jerked back up when Lady Fosberry cleared her throat, and she found her ladyship's keen gaze on her, as if she could see right through her.

Tilly caught her breath.

She *knew*. Lady Fosberry knew Kit's story for the lie it was.

But she didn't say a word. She only stared at Tilly, her head cocked to the side, her expression unreadable.

Lord Fairmont wasn't so inscrutable, however. "You expect me to believe, Prestwick, that both you and Miss Mathilda just happened to be in the rose garden at the same time Lord Wyle—whom I'll remind you I neither saw, nor heard—was attempting to kidnap my sister? Rather a stunning coincidence, isn't it?"

"Coincidental yes, but true all the same. Who the devil do you suppose ripped my arm to shreds, if not Wyle?" Kit held up his bloody arm. "Do you suppose your sister hit me with the riding crop?"

The very suggestion that sweet, gentle Harriett would strike anyone was ludicrous, but Lord Fairmont remained unmoved. "Certainly she would, if she was forced to defend herself. I'd sooner believe that than the lies you've told tonight."

"I'm not lying, Fairmont. If you don't believe me, ask your sister herself when she awakes. She'll tell you the same thing. I realize you're distraught, but if you'd take a moment to think, you'll see there's no reason in the world for me to abscond with Lady Harriett."

"Is that so? Because I can think of fifty thousand reasons why you—"

"I don't need your bloody money, Fairmont!" Kit gritted out between clenched teeth. "Even if I did, I wouldn't have to kidnap her to marry her. We were

179

promised to each other years ago. You arranged the match yourself. Or have you forgotten?"

"I've forgotten nothing. Not the agreement between us, and not the letter that was waiting for me when I returned to Fairmont House earlier this week —the letter that announced your intention to court my sister this season."

Kit threw his hands up into the air. "And what of it? I did intend to court her when I first arrived in London, but then..." He glanced at Tilly. "I changed my mind. Lady Harriett is lovely, but we don't suit."

"At last, a point we can agree on." Lord Fairmont let out a grim laugh. "I wonder though, Prestwick, if you really did change your mind, or if Harriett refused you? Or perhaps you heard I was returning to England, and you knew I'd never approve the match when I discovered what a scoundrel you are. So, you decided to take matters into your own hands—"

"James!" Lady Fosberry snapped. "That is quite enough. Christopher is telling the truth. He never initiated a courtship with Harriett. Indeed, it's Lord Wyle who's been courting her all season. Before you hurl any more unfounded accusations, I advise you to wait until Harriett awakes. She'll tell you herself that—"

"It doesn't matter what Harriett says. A half dozen servants witnessed the scene in the drive this evening. By tomorrow morning, all the *ton* will know of it. She's disgraced now."

"My servants can be trusted not to breathe a word of what they saw tonight," Lady Fosberry said, but her face had gone pale. "We'll make certain—"

"No, Aunt. That's not good enough." Lord Fairmont turned to Kit. "There's only one way to set this right. Prestwick here is going to marry Harriett."

Kit, marry Harriett? Tilly sucked in a breath. Kit's gaze snapped to hers, but he looked away quickly. "You're mad, Fairmont."

"If you refuse, Prestwick, then I will have no choice but to demand satisfaction from you for the insult you've dealt my sister."

At that, Kit leapt to his feet, his calm deserting him. "For God's sake, Fairmont—"

"Is that a refusal, Prestwick?"

This time, when Kit looked at Tilly, he didn't look away, and she... she couldn't. In that moment, nothing in the world could have torn her gaze from his. A heartbeat passed, then another, his beautiful dark eyes soft and warm as he gazed at her. "It is a refusal," he said at last, still holding her eyes. "I don't love your sister, Fairmont. I'm in love with Tilly, and she's the lady I'm going to marry."

Oh, dear God. Dear *God*—

"*Tilly!*" Phee shot to her feet with a gasp. "I... you... you're in love with Tilly? You intend to *marry* Tilly?"

"Very well then, Prestwick." Lord Fairmont tossed back his brandy, and slammed the tumbler down on a table. "Primrose Hill at dawn, the day after tomorrow."

"You're acting in haste, Fairmont—"

"Appoint your second. I'll receive him here tomorrow morning."

"You're making a mistake, Fairmont. We're *friends*—"

"No, we're not. Not anymore." Lord Fairmont

turned and left the drawing room without another word, leaving them all speechless behind him.

All but Kit, who hurried to Tilly, and took her hands. "I didn't intend to offer my hand to you in quite this way, but I love you, Tilly. Will you have me?"

Have him? Had he not heard Lord Fairmont? The Prestwick curse was true, and it was unfolding right before their eyes! Through no fault of his own, a most improbable series of events were lining up in a most improbable way to see Kit sent to the dueling field!

Couldn't he see that? In two days, he'd be murdered in a duel! There was no question the encounter would end with a pistol ball embedded in his flesh. The curse would see to that. It would make certain he—

"Tilly?" He took her hand. "Do you love me?"

She could only gaze up at him, her heart fluttering like a trapped bird inside her chest. She was twenty-one years old, and in that time, she'd never once imagined she might marry someday. She'd always intended to live out her days in Hambleden with Phee. She'd never indulged in girlish fantasies of a gentleman who'd steal her heart, and make her his bride.

But she hadn't planned on Kit, had she? Whoever would have imagined she'd fall madly in love with a rake? But here she was, with her heart torn to shreds, and every hope she'd never known she had falling to ruins.

Because she *did* love him. So much, her heart ached with it every time she looked into his dark eyes, and every time he smiled at her. She'd never imagined there could be such a love as what she felt for him.

And that was why she had to refuse him.

"Tilly?"

"I can't...marry you, Kit."

She tried to withdraw her hands, but he caught them, and pressed them first to his lips, then to his chest, over his heart. "That's not what I asked you, Tilly. I asked if you love me."

"That doesn't matter." It should matter—it should be the only thing that mattered—but it seemed the Prestwick curse had caught her in its talons, and it was squeezing her, ripping into her flesh. "I won't send you to the dueling field to die, Kit."

"There will be no duel, Mathilda."

They all turned to stare at Lady Fosberry.

"Once Harriett awakens," her ladyship went on, "She'll tell her brother the truth, and this mess will be set to rights. James is shocked and distraught right now, but he's not an unreasonable man. He'll come to his senses, I promise you. If you do love Christopher, Mathilda, then accept his hand, and allow yourself to be happy."

"Do you love him, Tilly?" Phee asked, seeming to hold her breath. "Are you in love with Lord Prestwick?"

"I told you, it doesn't matter." Couldn't they see it didn't matter? "He'll wed Harriett, just as Lord Fairmont demands. They've long been promised to each other, and I think... I think it was meant to turn out this way all along. Lord Fairmont is right—it's the only way to save Harriett from scandal."

She couldn't let her tender-hearted friend face the scorn of the *ton*.

But it was more than that. So much more.

Even if Kit would never be hers, she couldn't bear to lose him.

A marriage to Hariett was the only way to save him from a painful, bloody death, and then there was the child, Samuel, to consider. What would become of him if Kit... if Kit...

"I—I'm sorry." She raised Kit's hand to her lips, and pressed a brief kiss to his palm. "I'm sorry."

"Tilly, wait!" Kit called after her, his voice breaking, and that...oh, God, it shattered her heart into a thousand pieces to walk away from him, but she didn't return to the drawing room, take his hands, and tell him she *did* love him, and would be his forever, because if she looked into the dark eyes that made her heart pound, and butterflies batter against her rib cage...

She'd be lost.

And in two days' time, he would be as well, his body lying bloodied and broken on Primrose Hill just like his uncle's before him, a victim of a curse that didn't distinguish between the innocent and the guilty.

She could never doom him to such an ugly fate. She wouldn't, even if it meant she must give him up. So, she fled up the stairs without a backward glance, tears scalding her eyes, and Kit's desperate pleas echoing in her ears.

CHAPTER
SIXTEEN

"Tilly? Wake up, dearest."

A gentle hand was shaking Tilly's shoulder, but she squeezed her eyes closed as tightly as her eyelids would allow. Last night had been torturous. She'd tossed and turned in her bed until the moon had traded places with the first meek rays of the sun, and when she had managed to fall into a fitful sleep, she'd been haunted by Kit's voice calling to her, and the memory of his dark eyes filled with sadness.

She didn't *want* to wake up. Nothing but heart-break awaited her.

But Phee, who'd never been one to be easily deterred when it came to her sisters' wellbeing, gave her another nudge. "Come, Tilly. I know you're unhappy, but we really must talk."

There was no avoiding it, was there?

She let out a long sigh and peeled her eyelids away from her sore, gritty eyes. "We said everything that needed to be said last night." How few words it had taken, to destroy the happiness of so many people! "I don't see what's left to talk about."

185

Her voice was hoarse from weeping, and her tone not at all friendly, but Phee overlooked it with the unending patience of a lady burdened with five younger sisters. "Did we? Because I was under the impression we'd only just begun."

Yes, and that beginning had left a long, jagged scar on her heart. If they delved any deeper, she'd bleed to death. "Rather a painful start."

Phee wisely ignored this as well and reached behind her to plump the pillows. "Sit up, dearest. Yes, that's better." She retrieved a tray from the table and placed it on Tilly's lap. "Here you are."

Tilly stared down at the pot of tea and the plate of toast. "I'm not hungry." She sounded like a sulky child, but there would be no choking down any toast or tea today.

Phee said nothing, only busied herself arranging the tea things, pouring out a cup of tea and setting it into the saucer. "Perhaps just a sip of tea?"

Tilly let out a beleaguered sigh, but she raised the cup to her lips, her gaze wandering toward Harriett's bed. She'd expected to find her friend curled into a ball of misery, but the bed was empty, the coverlet neatly smoothed over the pillow. "My goodness, what's become of Harriett? Is she—"

"Harriett is fine, or as well as can be expected, given her ordeal last night. Lady Fosberry came and fetched her earlier this morning. The two of them were closeted in her ladyship's private parlor when I came upstairs. They've been in there for hours."

Goodness, poor Harriett. Tilly didn't envy her that confrontation. There weren't enough hours in the day for her to explain how she'd ever agreed to Lord Wyle's mad scheme in the first place. Lady Fosberry wielded considerable power over the *ton*, but even she couldn't set such a mess as this to rights.

But then, she wouldn't have to, would she? Harriett would marry Kit, and it would be as if that terrifying encounter with Lord Wyle had never hap—

"How long have you been in love with Lord Prestwick, Tilly?"

Tilly spluttered, the sip of tea she'd just taken spraying with alarming force from her lips. "I—I'm not...not—"

"Yes, you are. I can tell just by looking at you. I only wonder I didn't see it sooner."

Oh, when would she learn that Phee, for all her quiet reserve, never missed a thing? She was the most dangerously perceptive lady in all of England. There was no sense in trying to keep anything from her, and Tilly didn't want to. She needed her sister, and anyway, look at what all her secrets had gotten her! Nothing but misery, and a night rail stained with tea.

"Come, Tilly." Phee took her hand. "Let's not have any more secrets between us, alright?"

"I didn't mean to fall in love with him! I didn't even want to! It just happened. It's most unfair, really."

"There are no rules in love, Tilly. It has its way, in the end."

"But it hasn't had its way! Don't you see? Kit is going to marry Harriett."

"I wouldn't be so sure of that."

Tilly tried to hold back the tears that threatened, but Phee's voice was so gentle, and her expression so kind, and Tilly's lips were already trembling, and it was no use, was it?

She was going to cry. *Again.*

"Oh, my dear." Phee plucked up the cloth from the tray and dabbed at the tears on her cheeks. "I have a notion things will work out as they're meant to, but why didn't you simply tell me you were in love?"

There was no mistaking the hurt in Phee's eyes, and Tilly's stomach twisted. "I didn't know at first, and then later... I never imagined I'd marry Kit, or anyone else. I never intended to marry, so there didn't seem to be any point in worrying you over it."

"You came to London for a season, but never intended to marry? I don't understand, Tilly. I thought you *wanted* to marry."

"No. I only came for Harriett."

"But why should you not want to marry? I know you find Hambleden confining. Indeed, Tilly, my greatest hope for you this season was that you'd fall in love, and have wonderful adventures."

Tilly stared down at her hands, plucking nervously at the coverlet. "I don't want to leave you alone, Phee."

"Me?" Phee sounded astonished. "I'm not alone, Tilly. I have you, and Emmeline, Juliet and Helena. I can visit any of you at any time—"

"But you never do, Phee! Or at least, not often. You spend most of your time in Hambleden, and now you'll be there alone, and I can't bear it. None of us can! We don't want you to be lonely—"

"Shhh. It's alright, dearest." Phee gathered her into her arms. "I promise I'll do better. Will that make you feel better?"

"Yes, but you must keep your promise." Tilly sniffled against Phee's shoulder.

"I will, I swear it. Now, is there anything else you've been keeping from me?"

"No, and I never will again. The last thing I want to do is cause another dreadful scandal—"

"Scandal?" Phee frowned. "You never caused any scandal."

"Yes, I did." Why did Phee keep forgetting? "The scandal with Miss Groves—"

"That blasted Miss Groves!" Phee's hands curled into fists. "I could happily wring her neck!"

Violence, from *Phee*? Goodness, she'd never seen such a thing before. "It was my fault, Phee—"

"It most certainly was not your fault! How can you think so, Tilly?"

"Because I attract scandal, Phee! I don't mean to, but I seem to fall from one scrape into another. I swore to myself I'd avoid another mishap when we came to London, but it's no use! This business with Lord Wyle is sure to come back on us, and I'll have embarrassed you again, and made you ashamed of me."

"Ashamed of you?" Phee stared at her, her mouth open in shock. "Where did you get that idea? I've never been ashamed of you a day in my life, Tilly!"

"But you must be!" The words were spouting like a fountain from her lips now, and there was no stopping them, no stemming the tide. "I'm not like you, or Emmeline, or Juliet or Helena. I'm not clever, or charming, or... or... I take after our mother—"

"Stop! Dearest, you must stop! None of this is true. You *are* clever, kind and loving, and so brave and fierce! Why, I wish I had a tenth of your courage! I see now I haven't said it often enough, but I'm extraordinarily proud of you, Tilly."

Tilly sniffled. "You are?"

"*Yes*, dearest. So proud. I don't wonder at all that Lord Prestwick fell in love with you." Phee cocked her head to the side, considering. "Or you with him, come to that. He *is* very handsome."

"He is, isn't he?" No one with the gift of sight could ever deny Kit was handsome. "He's quite the most handsome gentleman I've ever seen, but I never intended to go as addle-pated over him as every other young lady in London." It was a trifle embarrassing, really, especially for a lady who'd sworn she'd never fall in love.

"I daresay you wouldn't have if he had only his looks to recommend him, but that's not the case. Last night, when he declared his love for you to everyone in the room? My goodness, I nearly swooned." Phee patted her chest. "I don't see why everyone insists that he's such an awful rake. I think he's lovely."

"He isn't a rake at all, Phee! He's truly the dearest, loveliest man imaginable."

Phee smiled. "Spoken like a lady in love. As I said, love will have its way in the end."

But Tilly wasn't so sure. Everything was in such a dreadful tangle! "Will it, Phee? Will it truly?"

"It will, I promise you." Phee squeezed her hand. "Just wait and see."

～

"WELL, FAIRMONT, WE MEET AT LAST." Darby dropped into a chair in front of Lord Fairmont's desk. "Prestwick's always spoken highly of you." He ran a bored gaze over Fairmont, who was seated on the other side. "I confess I expected more."

Kit opened his mouth to warn Darby to keep a civil tongue in his head, but then closed it again without saying a word. Fairmont had made it clear he no longer considered Kit his friend, and after the accusations he'd hurled at him last night, he didn't owe the man any courtesy.

There was no silencing Darby when he was in a mood, in any case, and he was most certainly in a mood this morning. They'd presented themselves at Fosberry House, as Fairmont had demanded, and been ushered into the study, where they found Fairmont alone, his second nowhere to be seen.

"I can understand why you might initially suspect Prestwick here, Fairmont. His reputation is a bit tarnished."

"I thought you were on my side, Darby," Kit muttered.

Darby crossed one leg over the other knee. "I'm getting to that part. It's a pity that the Nonesuch turned out to be such a scoundrel, although I confess I suspected him from the start. The most perfect fruit always hides the worm, eh, Fairmont? Now Prestwick here may be a bit blighted on the outside, but his core is solid."

Good Lord, what an analogy. "Er, thank you, Darby. I think."

"I think only of my sister, and protecting her reputation," Fairmont said, but the fury that had so animated him last night had cooled, leaving him looking flat and exhausted.

"A bit late for that." Darby waved a dismissive hand in the air. "You might consider challenging the man who actually insulted her, instead of going after

Prestwick. Anyone can see he's head over heels for that Templeton chit. It's rather pathetic, really."

Kit rolled his eyes. "Thank you again, Darby."

"Just leave it to me, Prestwick. Now, Fairmont. If you insist on going through with this absurd duel, then you'll be facing off with *me*. We can't put Prestwick on the dueling field with that bloody curse hanging over his head, now can we?"

"What?" Kit jumped to his feet. "What the devil, Darby? You're not dueling in my place!"

"Hush, will you, Prestwick? Let Fairmont speak. Well, Fairmont?"

"I may have spoken too hastily last night, Prestwick," Fairmont began, "I shouldn't have accused you of—"

"James Abner Theophilus Fairmont!" A female voice cried, followed by footsteps in the corridor.

Darby turned to Kit, one eyebrow raised. "Theophilus?"

There was a scuffle in the hallway, and an instant later the door of the study flew open. Lady Harriett marched in, her cheeks bright, and eyes ablaze. "Lady Fosberry has just informed me that you've challenged Lord Prestwick to a duel!"

Fairmont rose from his chair. "This doesn't concern you, Harriett—"

"Oh yes, it does! Lord Prestwick never touched a single hair on my head. For pity's sake, James, he *saved* me last night. He, and Tilly. Not just my virtue, but perhaps even my life!"

Fairmont paled. "Hattie—"

"I despise duels, James, but if you insist upon dueling with someone, then it must be Lord Wyle. He's the culprit here, not Lord Prestwick."

Kit had never seen a man look more haggard, more beaten than James Fairmont did then. He was so white, so still, he might have been a wax figure. "I never should have left you alone, Hattie," he whispered. "None of this would have happened if I'd remained in England."

Lady Harriett's face softened, and she reached for her brother's hand. "You didn't leave me alone, James. You left me with our Aunt, and she's been very good to me. What happened with Lord Wyle was entirely my own fault. I never should have agreed to—"

"Let's not discuss it here, Hattie."

Fairmont led his sister to the door, but before they left, he turned back to Kit. "I beg your pardon, Prestwick. I've wronged you, and I hope you can find it in yourself to forgive me someday." His gaze slid to Darby. "Yes, Mr. Darby. *Theophilus*. It's a family name."

"I've just left Tilly in the breakfast room, my lord," Lady Harriett added, smiling at Kit. "*Alone*."

Once they were gone, Darby rose to his feet. "Well, it looks as if my work here is done. No need to thank me, Prestwick."

"Yes, there is." Kit laid a hand on Darby's shoulder. "Thank you, Darby. You're a good man and a loyal friend."

"Shhh. For God's sake, Prestwick, someone will hear you." Darby winked. "Now, if you'll excuse me, I'm off to pay a call on Miss Edgerley."

"Is that so?" Kit followed Darby to the front door. "How uncharacteristically gallant of you."

"She's a dreadful harridan, you know, Prestwick, and doesn't find me at all charming. I like her immensely." Darby accepted his hat and stick from

Watkins, then grinned at Kit, and hurried out the door, calling over his shoulder. "Good luck with Miss Mathilda."

But Kit didn't need luck. He only needed Tilly. No luck, neither good nor bad, and no curse could ever touch him, as long as he had her.

She was right where Lady Harriett had said she'd be, alone in the breakfast room, an untouched cup of tea on the table before her. "Tilly."

Her head jerked up at the sound of his voice, and then... God above, the smile that rose to her lips made his knees go weak. He'd devote his entire life to making her smile if she'd only let him.

"Kit. I couldn't sleep for thinking of you."

She started to rise to her feet, but he hurried across the room and fell to his knees beside her chair. "Let's try this again, shall we? Properly, this time." He took her hands in his and drew in a deep breath. "Do you love me, Tilly?"

"Oh, *yes*. I do love you, Kit. So very much."

"I can't bear to let you go, Tilly. I want you with me forever, as my wife, my countess, and my love." He brought her hands to his lips. "Do you want me?"

"More than anything I've ever wanted in my life. More than I ever believed I could want someone." She cupped his face in her hands, her palms warm against his cheeks. "How could I not? Every young lady in London has gone mad for the handsome Earl of Prestwick."

"Ah, but he only wants one lady. Only one lady in all of England will do for him."

"Indeed? Is it one of the Misses Arundel?" she asked, her eyes twinkling.

God, how he adored her. "No. She's one of the

Misses Templeton. I've been madly in love with her since she nearly blinded me with absinthe. She was the first lady I saw when I opened my eyes afterward, and the only lady I've been able to see since."

She gazed down at him, her eyes as warm and blue as a summer sky. "The *ton* will say I've bewitched you."

"You *have*, Tilly." He wrapped his arms around her waist and rested his head in her lap, his eyes closing at the soft drift of her fingers playing in his hair. "You have."

EPILOGUE

LATE AUGUST, 1816 HAMPSTEAD HEATH, LONDON

"You don't think we're making a mistake, do you?" They'd just crossed the footpath that led from Prestwick House to Lady Fosberry's rose garden, but when they reached the gate, Tilly held back, her fingers tightening around Kit's hand.

"My dearest wife, you've asked me that same question a dozen times this morning, and I'll give you the same answer I did every other time." He tugged her into his arms and dropped a kiss on the end of her nose. "No, I don't, and even if we are, it's too late now. Lady Fosberry is waiting for us."

"It's easy enough for you to say so. You weren't there to witness the worst of his trickery, as I was." Still, despite her misgivings, she allowed Kit to maneuver her through the gate. "Why, there was a time or two I would have sworn he was pure evil."

"That may be, but surely as a Countess of Prestwick, you'd never hold the child responsible for the sins of his father?" He swung their hands playfully between them as they walked. "Or his grandfather, his brother, his uncle—"

"Hush." She pressed her fingers to his lips. "Of course not. You're quite right."

After the debacle with Harriett and Lord Wyle, there'd been no signs of the Prestwick curse. Indeed, they'd been so deliriously happy together, that Tilly chose to believe the ancient curse that had plagued the Prestwick family for so long had seen fit to reverse itself, and become a blessing, instead.

"Look, Kit. Some of Lady Fosberry's roses are still in bloom." From here, she could just make out a few deep pink and bright yellow blooms, like splashes of paint against the gray canvas of the late summer sky.

"So they are." He led her across the garden to the few remaining blossoms, smiling down at her as she pressed her nose to the petals and inhaled. "Very pretty indeed, Lady Prestwick. Perhaps we should grow roses in the hothouses this winter."

"What a wonderful idea." They'd lived in the cottage for some months after their wedding, and she could have happily remained there, but as the sharpest pain from his uncle's death had begun to fade, Kit had declared himself ready to take possession of Prestwick House.

So, they'd left Kent to come to London in the most unfashionable month of the year to open the house, baby Samuel tucked into his basket on the seat between them.

He'd been ever so good, too. He'd hardly cried at all, and he had the most darling red curls and the loveliest bright dark eyes. She couldn't look at him without smiling.

He was a most superior child, and a Prestwick, through and through.

"When do you suppose Harriett and Lord Fairmont will arrive?" Kit asked as they resumed their walk toward Fosberry House. "Did Harriett write?"

"She did. They expect to be here by the end of the month." She bit her lip. "I do hope her second season isn't an utter disaster, Kit. I can't bear to see her disappointed again."

"I know, love." He squeezed her hand. "I think she has a fair chance of making a decent match. It's fortunate we married so quickly. It helped distract the gossips from Harriett's, er, misstep with Wyle."

It was the truth. Lord Wyle hadn't been as fortunate, however. His shameful gaming debts had been exposed, and between that and the whispered rumors of his questionable behavior with Lady Harriett, the *ton* had quite turned on him. The last she'd heard, he'd retreated to the Continent, and had no plans to return to London.

But while Harriett had escaped relatively unscathed, the gossip about Tilly and her sisters had been deafening. "Dear me!" Tilly let out an exaggerated sigh. "Another of London's most sought-after noblemen, taken in by those dreadful Templeton sisters!"

Kit grinned. "Enchantresses, each and every one of them."

"Poor, dear Lord Prestwick." She shook her head. "I daresay he'll live to regret his choice."

"I daresay he won't." He caught her around the waist, pulled her close, and brought his mouth down on hers, teasing at the seam of her lips with a seductive stroke of his tongue.

She opened at once. He had quite the loveliest lips she'd ever tasted, and she never could resist his kisses.

They were so lost in each other, that neither of them heard the front door open until a loud "Ahem!" made them spring apart.

Lady Fosberry stood in the doorway, her hands on her hips and her eyebrows raised, looking very stern indeed, but for the smile twitching at her lips. "Really, Christopher, have you no self-control? And you, Tilly! Disgraceful. If the two of you would be so good as to unhand each other, we may proceed indoors."

"I beg your pardon, my lady." Kit led Tilly up the stairs and into the entryway. "You may blame Lady Prestwick, for being so irresistible."

"Shame on you, Christopher. Everyone knows the gentleman is always to blame for such things. Now come along, both of you. I can't wait to show them to you!"

"We can't wait to see them," Kit said as they followed Lady Fosberry into the entryway.

"Have you heard from Euphemia, Tilly?" Lady Fosberry asked as they made their way to the servants' back staircase. "I've written her, but I haven't heard a word in reply. I do hope she doesn't intend to change her mind about helping Harriett this season. I need her matchmaking expertise. I don't like to take any chances on London's noblemen after Lord Wyle turned out to be such a scoundrel."

"You needn't worry, my lady. Phee is in Oxfordshire at the moment, but she's promised to come for the entire season, and she will."

Phee had been as good as her word. Instead of languishing in Hambleden, she'd spent a month in London after their wedding, and since then she'd been flitting back and forth between Juliet and Helena in Oxfordshire, and Emmeline at Melrose

House in Kent, where she was a great favorite with Lord Melrose's three younger sisters. They'd all spent Christmas there together, and one would never have guessed, to see Phee's smiles and hear her laughter, that she was anything less than utterly content.

But a lady could never fool her sisters. For all her gaiety, loneliness seemed to cling to Phee still, and it was a loneliness none of them could help with, no matter how much they might want to, because it was a loneliness of the heart.

"Here we are." Lady Fosberry opened the door to the kitchen, and hurried over to a basket in the corner. "I keep them here, as it's the warmest place in the house. Aren't they the most precious things imaginable?"

As it turned out, Lucius had a reason for his sneaky visits to Prestwick Cottage. He was having a grand affair with a pretty white and tan King Charles Cavalier spaniel that had been one of Kit's Uncle Freddy's hunting dogs.

The result of this romance was nine wriggling, snuffling puppies, half of them white, like Lucius, and the other half with the same brown markings as their mother.

And there was one...

"Oh Kit, look!" Tilly knelt on the floor, reached into the basket and drew out a squirming body. The puppy was mostly white, but she—yes, she felt sure it was a *she*—had the most fetching brown starburst around one of her eyes. "Have you ever seen anything more beautiful?"

"I have, indeed." Kit smiled at her, his dark eyes twinkling. "But I own he's a very handsome dog. Or she's a very pretty one." He turned to Lady Fosberry. "Which is it?"

"Why, she's a girl, of course!" Tilly interrupted. "Can't you tell? Just look at that darling face!" She squealed as the puppy burrowed into the hollow between her neck and shoulder. "Look, she loves me already!"

"Of course, she does. Who wouldn't?" Kit glanced at Lady Fosberry. "Are you certain you're willing to part with her, my lady?"

"Yes, indeed. What am I to do with nine puppies? I'll just leave you two here to get acquainted with her, shall I?"

Lady Fosberry vanished up the stairs, and Kit sat down beside Tilly, stretched his legs out in front of him, and reached over to stroke the puppy's head. "Do you suppose she'll do?"

"Do? She's perfect, Kit." She leaned over, and pressed a kiss to his cheek. "You're perfect, too. Have I told you yet today?"

"You have, yes, several times." He watched her with the puppy for a while, then he slid closer, his thigh pressed against hers, and wrapped his arm around her. "From a family of three to a family of four, in the blink of an eye. Dear me, we are reckless, aren't we?"

Tilly rested her head on his arm. "I hope she's the first of many additions."

"Me too, love." He pressed a kiss to her forehead. "Me, too.

ALSO BY ANNA BRADLEY

ABOUT THE AUTHOR

Anna Bradley writes steamy, sexy Regency historical romance—think garters, fops and riding crops! Readers can get in touch with Anna via her webpage at http://www.annabradley.net. Anna lives with her husband and two children in Portland, OR, where people are delightfully weird and love to read.

ABOUT THE AUTHOR

Anna Bradley writes steamy, sexy Regency historical romance—think garters, fops and riding crops! Readers can get in touch with Anna via her webpage at http://www.annabradley.net. Anna lives with her husband and two children in Portland, OR, where people are delightfully weird and love to read.